The man frowned down at her. And he soun[...] irritated . . . but she was the one who'd gotten wet. She was the one who had a right to be upset.

"What the devil yourself!" She stood and glared at him. "I had this blasted floor mopped until you came along and made a mess of it. Now look at it. I'll have to do it all over. And look at me—there'll be no doing me over."

"You do look a bit . . . bedraggled." He wasn't just grinning; the arrogant son-of-a-sailor was almost laughing.

"This isn't funny. I'll have to redo the floor, instead of returning to the party where I'm supposed to be. My hair has to be fixed, and this dress—this dress is ruined."

"Again, I apologize. By the way, my name's Mike, and you're . . . ?"

"Ellie." Her smile twisted self-mockingly. "As in CinderEllie. All of a sudden, the name seems horribly apt."

Dear Reader:

Happy Valentine's Day!

It takes two to tango, and we've declared 1989 as the "Year of the Man" at Silhouette Desire. We're honoring that perfect partner, the magnificent male, the one without whom there would *be* no romance. January marks the beginning of a twelve-month extravaganza spotlighting one book each month as a tribute to the Silhouette Desire hero—our *Man of the Month*!

Created by your favorite authors, these men are utterly irresistible. Joan Hohl's Mr. February is every woman's idea of the perfect Valentine, and March, traditionally the month that "comes in like a lion, goes out like a lamb," brings a hero to match with Jennifer Greene's Mr. March.

Don't let these men get away!

Yours,

Isabel Swift
Senior Editor & Editorial Coordinator

NANCY GRAMM
High Jinx

Silhouette Desire

Published by Silhouette Books New York

America's Publisher of Contemporary Romance

SILHOUETTE BOOKS
300 East 42nd St., New York, N.Y. 10017

ISBN: 0-373-05479-3

First Silhouette Books printing February 1989

Printed in the U.S.A.

Books by Nancy Gramm

Silhouette Desire

Then Came Love #339
About Last Night . . . #422
High Jinx #479

NANCY GRAMM

comes from a long line of grit and promise, beginning with the ancestors who came to the New World from England in 1749 to grub a living in Alabaman soil.

The past 240 years have wrought a number of changes. Nancy doesn't grub in the soil, except occasionally in a flower bed. When she's not writing, she works as a communications consultant with a local telephone company and lives in the Dallas, Texas, area with her police detective husband, Tom, and their two cats: Spider, a short-haired alley cat, and a Maine coon cat named Murphy.

For Mama,
for teaching me that anything worth having
is worth fighting for,
and that reality can be better than dreams,
and for giving me my stepfather, Virgil Brown,
who laughed at life even as he labored in it.

With special thanks to Ava Biggs and Kay Rasco
for their assistance and support.

One

Mike Bannister slapped his pencil onto the balance sheet that was spread across his desk. There had to be some mistake; his company couldn't be in as bad shape as it looked on paper.

He frowned at the offending figures. He'd been over them too many times to discount them, but he could do nothing more about them tonight.

He crumpled the balance sheet into a ball and tossed it at the empty wastebasket next to his desk. It hit the edge, balanced precariously, then fell in. At least he still had his hook shot, he thought ruefully.

He'd have more than that if he could only bring in the Dunes well. Then he should be to able attract all the investors Bannister Drilling would need to bring it out of this slump.

He stood and crossed over to the window. From the second floor he could only see the scattered spotlights from the plaza below, which was just as well. Lately the lights of the city had seemed duller to him; they lacked glitter.

But one day Dallas would shine again for him, he promised himself—despite the balance-sheet figures, despite the success or failure of the well in Dunes, Arizona.

Thrusting his hands into his pockets, Mike leaned against the window frame. He knew that if he would only swallow his pride, he need never worry about money again. But he didn't consider begging an option. He refused to accept charity, no matter how lovingly it was offered. He would pull himself out of this mess, by himself.

He was certain there was oil, though so far the well had proven dry. He felt it with the same gut instinct that had guided him many times before. What he didn't know—what his gut couldn't tell him—was how far he'd have to drill to hit it.

Or whether he'd run out of money first.

His instincts told him to stay with it, and so many times in the past his instinct—salted with his geological training and a little luck—had spelled success for him on wildcat ventures such as this one.

He returned to his desk, settled one hip on the corner of it and sipped his coffee. Then he grimaced. The coffee was colder than sin and stronger than the devil. He'd have a hell of a time sleeping anyway, and he had to fly to Arizona tomorrow.

Tonight he could only leave his fate to Lady Luck.

Mike tossed his jacket over one shoulder, picked up his briefcase and left his office. Before he left town, he had to check with W.C., his driller, to get the latest mud sample results.

Then he'd have something to mull over during the flight tomorrow. Superstitious though it might be, he felt his being in Dunes would make a difference. Right now, he was too damn far away to affect anything.

The stairs in the Davis Building seemed to pour in a free-form fall of tile from the second floor to the center of the first. As Mike descended slowly, thoughtfully, he heard only the loud rumble of the lobby's waterfall.

Rounding the landing, he glanced at his watch. Even allowing time for the commute home, he ought to get a half-decent night's sleep.

On the second step below the landing, he kicked against a metal mop bucket. Swearing at the sharp pain that stabbed his foot, he watched helplessly as the bucket tilted, throwing a wave of dirty water forward before it flipped over and clattered down the stairs.

It had almost reached the bottom before Mike saw her. Kneeling at the foot of the stairs, the woman lifted her head, her disarrayed honey-blond hair swirling around her shoulders, her blue eyes large and startled.

For an instant his gaze held hers in a freeze-frame stare, until the remaining water splashed her and the bucket clipped her shoulder. Within him, sudden amusement battled with bewilderment as he saw what she was wearing. The lady wore a green plastic garbage bag.

* * *

Ellie Logan barely had time to think before the water hit her, spraying her face, splattering her hair and splashing down her to drench one corner of her purple silk hem. As if it were an afterthought, the bucket struck her.

It was the last straw, the capper to an evening gone bad.

"What the devil...?" The man frowned down at her, his face angular, its features sharp as if etched by an artist more aware of details than of the whole, a face in quiet conflict with itself.

And he sounded irritated...but she was the one who'd gotten wet. She was the one who should be aggravated.

"What the devil yourself!" Wiping her face with the back of her hand, she stood and glared at him. "I had this blasted floor mopped until you came along and made a mess of it. Now look at it; I'll have to do it all over. And look at me; there'll be no doing me over."

A touch of humor sparked his gray eyes and tautened the corners of his mouth. "You do look a bit...bedraggled."

"I'll give you bedraggled." When she stepped forward, something crunched beneath her heel. "Blast it." She lifted her stockinged foot off a tortoiseshell comb, its spine flattened, its teeth splayed. "I can't believe—look at this. Great-aunt Hilda gave this comb to me—it's older than I am."

"It looks it, too," he said with a grin. He set down his briefcase at the bottom of the stairs.

He wasn't just grinning, she reassessed. The arrogant son of a sailor was almost chortling.

"Why were you on your hands and knees anyway?" he asked.

"Trying to *find* Aunt Hilda's comb," she snapped. "I'd dropped it." She shoved a soggy strand of hair behind her ear. "And this isn't funny. I'll have to redo the floor, instead of returning to the party where I'm supposed to be."

She'd still be at the party if the employee who regularly cleaned the lobby hadn't gone into labor two months early. Ellie had had no choice but to leave Robert's dinner party. Temporarily, she'd believed, which was why she'd protected her dress as best she could with the plastic garbage bag. The drive to change into suitable clothes to finish the job would have taken time she hadn't had.

"And I'm driving Robert's Porsche," she suddenly realized, her voice lifting in what was almost a wail. "I can't go back to his elegant party like this—and it's all your fault."

"You're right," he said soothingly, moving beside her, his voice as rich and thick and spiced as a cup of Mexican chocolate. "It is my fault, and I apologize. But I can help."

She laughed disparagingly. "My hair has to be redone, and this dress—" she gestured toward her drooping hem "—this dress is ruined."

"Even bedraggled, you look enchanting. And how long could it take to dry you off?" Cocking his head, he studied her inquisitively. "I don't want to be rude, but I have to ask. Is there some reason for this?'' He plucked at the armhole she'd cut in the garbage bag.

"Of course there is," she said indignantly. "I'm supposed to be at a very elegant party."

"How stupid of me; I should've known that."

"I mean, the bag was supposed to protect my dress. And it would have except for—"

"For me?"

"You and your dropkick," she allowed.

"Again, I apologize. By the way, my name's Mike, and you're . . . ?"

"Ellie." Her smile twisted self-mockingly. "As in CinderEllie. All of a sudden the name fits horribly."

"Wrong adverb. It fits magically," he said. "How long is this elegant party supposed to last?"

"Not nearly long enough." She lifted her sodden hem and winced. "Even Walt Disney himself couldn't fix this quick enough."

When she glanced up, his penetrating gray eyes held her blue ones captive. She shivered involuntarily, almost instinctively.

"First of all," he said, "you need to think more positively. Your coverall protected most of you. And I have a hair dryer in my office bathroom that'll take care of most of the rest."

"But I still have to mop—"

"Don't worry about the floor. I'll have it taken care of." He picked up her cracked hair comb and slid it into his pocket, then he retrieved his briefcase and led her up the stairs, sidestepping the patches of wet. "I've never met anyone from a fairy tale before," he said. "Was it magic that got you here from the ball?"

"Hardly. You could say I came in the prince's Porsche...only I didn't. The Porsche belongs to my friend Robert."

"Robert's not a prince?"

"Not mine. Besides, do I look like princess material to you right now?"

He swept a long, misty gaze over her. "You know, I think you do. I'd call any man who couldn't see it blind."

Standing next to him on the landing, Ellie felt an unreasoning panic rise in her. He wasn't a great deal taller than her five feet eight inches, but his presence was commanding. Though she didn't have to tilt her head to meet his gray eyes, gazing into them dwarfed her, made her feel small enough to crawl inside those black pupils. His eyes mesmerized her, stole her control.

She took a half step away from him, fighting the urge to flee. Instead she gave in to her nervous habit— she talked.

"Actually Robert has a princess. He just lent me his car because I'd taken a taxi to the party. My car's in the shop, you see, and the van isn't...elegant, and I'd helped him with the hors d'oeuvres...." She paused, took a deep breath and shut up. Sometimes when she rambled to cover her nervousness, she revealed entirely too much.

"You never did say how long the party would last," Mike reminded her.

His words were ordinary, and suddenly so were his eyes. Her apprehension receded.

"I'm not sure. What time is it? Close to eleven? It should be over in a couple of hours. I'll never make it."

"Sure you will," he said as they reached the top of the stairs. "There's probably some spot cleaner in my secretary's desk. With that and the hair dryer and..." He looked skeptically at her feet. "Cinderella left only one slipper with the prince. Both of your shoes are gone."

She wiggled a stockinged toe. "They were too delicate to work in, so I left them downstairs."

She decided there was more to Mike than showed on the surface. There was something synergistic about him, making the total effect of him far stronger than the sum of his individual parts—greater than his dark, curly hair by itself, more than just his olive skin tone or the lines etched into the corners of his eyes: more, even, than the laugh lines that edged his mouth.

She fought her physical attraction to him, fought it with inconsequential words. "You were frowning before," she said. "Was something bothering you?"

"Before?"

"Before the tidal wave. Before the mop bucket."

He shrugged. "I was just mulling over a small business problem. Correction, a big problem. But it should work out all right, with a little luck." His laugh lines deepened with his smile. "Got any to spare?"

She harrumphed. "Remember me? I was on the receiving end of that mop bucket."

"But Cinderella's magical. Everyone knows that. So how about a spell?"

"You forget—Cinderella was the bewitched, not the bewitcher."

He seemed to consider her statement. Then his expression lightened as if he'd solved all the ills of the world, and his laughter echoed in the empty hall, casting its own kind of spell. "Tell you what, Ellie. I'll cast one for you if you'll cast one for me."

"You're not serious."

"As a heart attack," he said.

"You're also crazy. And you know what? So am I. I'll do it if I can choose the spell you do for me—and I want to be abracadabraed. So, I'll bibbity bobbity boo you. Okay? Okay, then." She paused, considering, then began, "Mares eat oats and does eat oats and...mmm..." Amusement tinged her voice as she chanted. "Mike needs something lucky?"

Her amusement became a chuckle, giving her words the bounce of a gurgling stream. "Put them together and what have you got. Bibbity bobbity...buckey?"

He groaned.

"It *was* off-the-cuff," she said defensively. "But did it work? Do you feel any less like a frog?"

"As I recall, that's a different fairy tale altogether. But I can safely say that right now—" he checked his watch "—at 10:55, I've probably never felt less like a frog."

He didn't look like one, either, as he unlocked an oak door and swung it open. The suite they entered could have been a spread from *Architectural Digest*: luxurious, with dark wood, russet upholstery, elegant statuary, lush green plants and a mahogany desk, which Mike rummaged through until he unearthed a container of spot cleaner.

Then he led her into another office, this one more functional in appearance, with paper stacked evenly atop the desk.

He motioned to an adjoining bathroom. "There are towels in the cabinet over the toilet and a hair dryer under the sink. And if you'll tell me where you left your shoes, I'll get them."

"Wait a minute," Ellie objected. "What happened to *my* spell?"

He shook his head. "Sweetheart, my luck's so bad right now, any spell I cast would probably backfire."

She wasn't the least bit superstitious, but she *had* risked making a fool of herself with his blasted spell. "A bargain's a bargain," she argued. "You owe me one."

"Don't say I didn't warn you," His expression grew thoughtful. "Okay. Abra." He paused. "Cadabra. Now for the magic phrase..." He waved his hands with a flourish. "Addis Ababa Genghis Khan." Then, chuckling, he announced, "Your spell is cast."

"And I thought *mine* was ridiculous!"

"I warned you," he said. "Now, where are your shoes?"

"They're in the—" She hesitated. She'd enjoyed their repartee immensely.

But although tonight felt magical, Ellie had learned as a child that magic was a myth. She had accepted the real world where dreams weren't merely dreamt; they were built with a great deal of hard work.

"Your shoes," Mike prompted her.

"O-oh. Yes. They're in the…in the janitor's closet downstairs."

"Exactly where downstairs?"

"Do you know where the telephone room is? The janitor's closet is three doors down that same hall."

"Be back in a minute, then. And if you need anything while I'm gone, just step into the hall and whistle."

"I can't whistle, but I won't need to."

"You never learned to whistle? What kind of a kid were you, anyway?"

"Whistling isn't mandatory, you know. It wasn't then, and it's not now."

"Well, it's still not too late to learn," he said as he left. "I could teach you in no time."

Ellie watched the door close behind him, stared for several seconds at the oak panel. He was probably an expert whistler, she thought, most likely an expert of many things.

But somehow she believed she'd be better off in the long run not knowing the extent of his expertise.

"Can't find your shoes," Mike called as he reentered the office fifteen minutes later.

He hadn't located the janitor's closet, either. Three doors down from the telephone room he'd found an electrical closet; next to that, a real-estate office. Both had been locked.

He listened to the steady drone of the hair dryer from the bathroom. Apparently Ellie hadn't heard him. So he settled himself on his chair and propped his feet on the desk.

While he'd searched, he'd speculated as well. She was obviously employed by the janitorial company that cleaned the building, though she surely didn't work with the crew, considering the way she was dressed, Robert's Porsche and her elegant dinner party.

But whoever she was, before Ellie left tonight he intended to learn more about her. Because of her, he'd completely forgotten his need for sleep and the urgency of tomorrow's early flight—even the devastation a dry well would have on his business.

He pulled Great-aunt Hilda's comb from his pocket and examined it. It was obviously old, most likely brittle, and he wasn't sure it could be bent back into shape. But the crystals in the spine still glittered, catching the overhead light and casting it back in blue and green sparkles.

Like Ellie's eyes.

She was certainly taking a long time drying her hair. Granted, it was thick and almost shoulder length. But—he pushed back the cuff of his blue oxford shirt and checked the time—she'd been in the bathroom for at least twenty minutes.

He crossed over to the door. "Ellie?" He knocked, then moved his head closer.

No answer.

"Ellie?" he repeated in a louder voice. He heard only the steady buzz of the hair dryer.

Twisting the knob, he opened the door. The room was empty. The hair dryer lay abandoned on a folded hand towel, its heated breath blowing at the mirror over the vanity.

Ellie had sent him on a wild goose chase into the heart of the building, away from the exits, then walked out on him, without a word. Only the running hair dryer and the wet floor downstairs remained as proof that she was real and not a fantasy he'd conjured up in his fatigue.

Filled with an odd sense of disappointment, he turned off the hair dryer and left.

Half an hour later, Mike entered his house, slung his briefcase onto the sofa and loosened his tie.

He was tired, bone-tired. And, as he often did when he was tired, he pulled his saxophone from its case. Then, standing before a window, he serenaded the night with the blues.

Ellie had been real, not a fairy-tale princess or a goddess in disguise. And when she'd left, she'd taken nothing of his with her. He was the same man, with the same worries and the same dreams.

Still, he felt different, as if she had given something instead. Something he'd yearned for without ever realizing it. She had given it, then taken it with her. Still a residue remained.

Now his sax cried for him, not for Ellie. He made it weep for the small boy who'd felt fatherless, though he wasn't. As he'd done many times before, he forced his pain out through the horn, giving vent to feelings he never displayed otherwise.

When he'd blown the last throaty notes from the sax, Mike lowered it, then lowered his head for a moment, too. After a few minutes he breathed in and straightened, his exhaustion somehow less. No catharsis was as complete for him as playing.

He put away his horn and flicked on his answering machine, paying scant attention to the messages as he fixed himself a drink.

His mother wanted him to come for dinner. "Your father," she informed him in her rich, deep voice, "is going out of town next week, and he'd like to see you before he leaves." Then he listened to Alline, two-dates-and-he'd-had-enough Alline, who asked in her squeaky voice if she'd made him angry.

She hadn't. She was just *misproportioned* for Mike. He put more stock in a woman's intellect than in the dimensions of her chest.

Despite his saxophone, the haunting memory of honeysuckle and summer skies still nagged at him, a memory of halcyon moments that surely would be gone by tomorrow. His fingers closed around Great-aunt Hilda's comb in his trouser pocket as he listened to the punctuating click of the recorder between messages.

"Hope you're sitting down, Bannister," W.C.'s scratchy voice warned, and Mike clenched the comb.

Silence followed. It could be good news; it could be bad. W.C. always used pauses for dramatic effect.

Mike's irritation level rose. "Get on with it, dammit," he muttered.

"It happened at 10:56 tonight," W.C. drawled. "The Dunes popped. We brought it in." Then the driller whooped. "We did it, son. We finally brought that son of a wildcatter in." In the background the crew burst into rowdy laughter, obviously celebrating.

Mike whooped, too, his face splitting into a raw grin. If he'd had a hat on, he would have thrown it...thrown it so damned high it would've been stringing clouds on its way back down. He was hatless, so instead he executed a leap a cheerleader would have envied, then danced a jig into the kitchen. After pouring a bowl of Wheaties and milk and sprinkling it with a handful of raisins, he sat at the breakfast bar. In Mike's mind, he didn't dine on cereal and milk; he feasted on imagination and luck, on ambrosia, sustenance of the gods. When he was finished, he propped his elbow on the countertop and cupped his chin in his hand.

At 10:56. He grinned...one more time. It sounded like a lucky number to him.

Suddenly his expression sobered—10:56—about a minute after Ellie had chanted her whimsical bibbity bobbity boo.

He pulled her comb from out of his pocket, pitched it up in the air and caught it.

How about that? Lady Luck had returned, in the form of a cleaning lady.

Two

Ellie shifted the gears of the orange delivery van and tamped her rising irritation. Why the Chapmans had insisted on choosing the Hotel Regina for their silver-anniversary party was one of the not-so-sweet mysteries of life. Ellie had tried to point out that all preparation would have to be made during rush hour, which necessitated the navigation of Central Expressway during a time when traffic moved sporadically, if it all.

But the Chapmans hadn't minded; they didn't have to drive it. Their main reason for choosing the Genies to oversee this project might have been because of their acquaintance with Ellie's grandfather, but they obviously trusted the company's capabilities as well.

Finally the traffic began to move. Ellie placed a protective hand in front of the massive flower arrangement on the seat beside her and trod on the accelerator. Like a sleeping giant slowly roused, the van crept forward into the widening space between it and the Cadillac ahead.

Then a blue BMW whipped in front of her. She glowered at it and tapped her brakes, but her hand stopped the flowers from sliding so that no damage was done. And Central flowed, as erratically as ever.

Tonight's party had been a break for Ellie. In the beginning, the odd-job company she and her college roommate had formed three years ago had captured Dallas clients with its claim of "No jobs too odd for Genies, the odd-job company." The slogan had all the bravado the city on the Trinity River admired, and the Genies had prospered . . . in the beginning.

Recently business had leveled off and then it started to sink. Not completely, but enough to cause Ellie a sleepless night or two.

But a few of her recent restless nights couldn't be blamed on the business. The touch of whimsy that had led her to disappear from Mike's office last Friday had carried her through the first few days. But lately the echo of their shared laughter had begun to tease her— that and the memory of a man who'd drawn from her a different Ellie, a sharper, more vibrant person.

At least he'd kept his word and had the floor finished for her. For that she was thankful. She'd never reneged on a contract, much less one as critical as the Davis Building.

Maybe the Chapman party would prove the shot in the arm the Genies needed. *If* she could pull it off without a hitch...and without her partner, Swan, who had the flu.

Finally removing her hand from the flowers, Ellie flexed her shoulders and began to hum softly. She could handle the party, even without Swan. She could do anything, almost . . . anything, at least, that might be required tonight.

She eased her foot down on the accelerator. Central was speeding up, a little anyway.

Mike tapped his fingers against the steering wheel of his white '57 Thunderbird and checked his rearview mirror. The truck behind him—a thundering mass of heaven only knew how many pounds of steel—had been tailgating him for the past three miles.

He should have chosen an alternate route this late in the afternoon. As a native, he knew how Central tried a driver's patience. It always had; it always would.

But he was committed now, with no exit in sight and a fire-breathing semi on his tail.

He cursed as he topped a rise and saw, over the hood of the yellow Datsun in front of him, where traffic had stopped dead still at the bottom of the incline.

The truck still hugged his bumper.

Adrenaline surged through him. Maybe he might *just* be able to...

He tromped the accelerator and cut into the next lane, squeezing the "bird" into a tight space in front of an orange delivery van.

Brakes screeched behind him, brakes screamed to his left. Then a high-pitched squeal merged with the grinding of metal. Mike glanced over his shoulder as the rig plowed into the yellow Datsun, scrunching the rear end toward the back seat like an accordion.

Mike blew out a thankful whistle. The Datsun wasn't horribly damaged, so he doubted anyone was injured. But if he hadn't gotten out of the way, if he'd been sandwiched between the rig and the Datsun... He shook his head. Maybe last week's good luck was holding.

The space he'd forced the T-bird into spread open, and he flowed with it, maintaining a half-car-length cushion between the BMW in front and the van behind him. Then, as he checked the rearview mirror, he caught a glare from the woman driver behind, her face framed by the fronds of a bird of paradise.

Her hands were clamped around a veritable tropical garden, in what could have qualified as a half-nelson hold. The honey-colored knot on top of her head sat off center, yet flared in the sunlight, almost as bright as the petals of the flowers surrounding her.

When the traffic surged forward, so did Mike. The orange van kept pace with him. Then the third lane opened and the van flashed into it, pulling up to pass Mike before darting onto the exit, and he shot another look at the driver.

It was Ellie. CinderEllie.

She'd saved his neck, brought him luck one more time.

Ellie left Central with more verve than care. "That cotton-picking, straw-chewing son of a biscuit eater!" she swore softly. Granted, he'd have been squashed meat if he hadn't cut in front of her, and she didn't begrudge the man his skin. But darn it, she'd nursed those flowers all the way from north Dallas, brooded over them like a mother hen, only to have them mutilated three blocks from her destination.

"And who knows how I'm going to fix them." She tapped a fist against her steering wheel as she waited for a traffic light to change. She wouldn't try to patch up the arrangement until she reached the Regina. She'd probably have to send out for some new stems; she could tell several were bent, if not snapped altogether.

The sky darkened to the west as a passel of storm clouds scudded in. The change mirrored Ellie's disposition.

Had she imagined that driver's resemblance to Mike from last Friday? Probably. She'd seen a similarity in the set of the jaw, a likeness in the slant of the nose. That, coupled with a comparable disaster, had sparked a memory; surely that was all.

And if it had been Mike? "Once was more than enough," she muttered. "If that *was*, he's worse than a jinx—he's a curse!"

She'd come out on the short end of the stick with him once already. And Ellie had had all the short ends in her life that she wanted.

* * *

That night she hovered near the center buffet table in the Regina ballroom. In the absence of Swan, Ellie had divided her time and energy between the kitchen and the ballroom.

So far the party had gone well. She'd reassembled the centerpiece quite effectively. Though less majestic, its new, compact design fanned the fronds into a flawless arc.

The ballroom was immense, its floors marble, its walls covered with pale silk. The women arrived wearing Russian sable and mink, chinchilla and golden fox, draped over dresses by Givenchy and Pucci; the men sported satin-lapeled tuxedos, pastel silk shirts and vibrant cummerbunds.

Laughter as soft as a waterfall overlay the soft strains of a dance band that was set up at one end of the room. In the center and at the other end, linen-draped tables held trays of hot and cold hors d'oeuvres. Formally clad waiters and waitresses carrying trays of champagne-filled glasses wended their way through the guests.

Obviously the hors d'oeuvres tasted as delicious as they looked, Ellie thought. The guests clustered around each of the serving tables.

Perhaps she should make sure the caterer had brought enough. Tactfully, she reminded herself. He had come highly recommended as far as his cooking skills were concerned, but she'd already seen signs of his temper.

She had walked barely a yard away from the table when she heard a woman's voice, sharp and carrying, say, "My God, those flowers look sick. What kind of an arrangement is that?"

Ellie's stomach plummeted as she turned toward the voice. She didn't intend to make excuses. She wasn't that foolish. She was simply curious.

Blond, midthirtyish and clad in beaded silk, the woman was surrounded by several other guests. And Mike, Ellie's nemesis, lounged at her side.

The same laughter-filled eyes she'd seen so often in her dreams this past week held Ellie where she stood—held her, pinned her, trapped her.

Suddenly she realized, almost as if he'd verbally confirmed it, that he'd been the driver of the T-bird on the freeway. She wasn't sure how she knew, perhaps simply seeing again the set of his jaw, the slant of his nose. Or maybe it was his damnable laughter.

The son of a wishbone understood what he'd cost her this afternoon, seemed even to realize everything she'd gone through trying to restore the centerpiece.

Dropping Ellie a wink, Mike said to the blonde, "I'm surprised you don't recognize the style, Laura. It's the newest thing from the Orient. Kamikaze, I think it's called."

"Michael, darling, don't tease," Laura scolded him.

"You really haven't heard of it, have you? That's odd. You always seem to know what's new and remarkable before anyone else does."

"You're not joking? Well, Allison O'Donnell did say something last week. You know she just returned from the Orient and she mentioned a new technique...."

"New technique, my great-aunt Hilda!" Ellie snorted softly, resuming her journey to the kitchen. "The only technique Michael, darling, knows anything about is blarney. Fast-talking, twaddle-blathering bunkum!"

And thank heavens for that. She could almost forgive him the trouble he'd caused her in the first place, simply because he'd redeemed her in the end.

Still grumbling, but this time spicing it with a chuckle, she pushed through a swinging door into the kitchen. Mike's companion was either awfully thick or awfully gullible. Ellie didn't mind which, as long as Laura bought Mike's nonsense.

Mike stood next to Laura in a windowed alcove away from most of the activity in the ballroom. She seemed to have fastened herself to him, clinging almost. While normally he wouldn't have had any problem unfastening himself, now was different; now he couldn't afford to offend either one of the Morgans.

He was still surprised at seeing Ellie here, almost as surprised as he'd been at his reaction to her earlier. His stomach had knotted, his chest had tightened, as if she were more than only an intriguing woman.

Of all the beautiful people in the ballroom tonight, she seemed strangely the most striking. She wore no jewels, neither on her neck nor her wrists. Somehow they would have detracted from her lightly freckled skin and honey-colored hair, which were both highlighted by a simple cream silk gown. She was as lovely as her surroundings and lovelier than most of the other women, for hers was an understated beauty.

Though she easily could be, somehow he didn't believe she was a guest. And that abominable arrangement on the center table, most likely the same one he'd massacred on Central this afternoon, seemed to bear him out.

"Isn't that your brother over there?" Laura asked, tightening her hold on Mike's arm.

He followed the line of her gaze to where a hefty, cotton-haired man with a mustache chatted with the hostess.

He'd assumed David would be here tonight, though he didn't like it. But if he avoided every affair that might throw him together with his antagonistic half brother, he wouldn't have much of a social life. A great deal of his business was conducted at parties like this one.

"You don't have too much to do with the Davis family, do you?" Laura asked.

"Not much. Didn't you say Buck would be joining us soon?"

"Too soon, most likely." She swirled the last of her wine in her glass. "Why won't you talk about them?"

"About whom?"

"The Davises."

"Nothing to talk about," he told her. "What time did Buck say he'd be here?"

"You're beginning to irritate me, Michael," she warned him. "Buck will be here when he gets here. And I certainly hope you two won't be discussing business."

"We'll make sure we don't bore you—" he chucked her under the chin in a gesture he knew would annoy her "—but we have to get some things cleared up before he leaves. He is still leaving tomorrow, isn't he?"

"Yes, he is," she said abruptly. Then her expression shifted, anticipation edging out vexation. "Perhaps we can get together while he's gone."

Not on your life, Mike thought. But he said, with a manufactured measure of regret, "I'm afraid not. When I have friends with wives as good-looking as you..." He shook his head, leaving his thoughts unfinished.

"Buck needn't know."

Buck Morgan stepped into the alcove. "Needn't know what?" He wrapped his stocky arm around his wife's shoulders and pressed a kiss onto her neck. "I almost didn't find you, love."

She appeared disconcerted only momentarily. "That should keep you from becoming overconfident, darling," she said with a laugh.

"Overconfidence is something I don't have to worry about, married to you," Buck complained good-naturedly. Then he greeted Mike. "We'll talk later, all right? Right now, I'm going to steer this lady around the room and see how many eyes turn green."

Mike was glad to see them go, even though his business with Buck was his primary reason for being here.

But the night was still young. And he had other business he could attend to.

* * *

The party continued to run smoothly, thanks to Ellie's constant attendance to it. This was the first party of this size the Genies had ever managed, and now she had to oversee it alone, thanks to Swan's illness. But, aside from the usual small disasters, nothing untoward had happened so far tonight. At least nothing that couldn't be righted with a little work.

Ellie prayed the night would stay smooth. She'd never wanted to rely on references from her grandfather, would have felt uncomfortable if the Chapmans had been close friends of Grandpapa's. But they were barely more than acquaintances, so the reference didn't quite feel like nepotism to Ellie.

As she walked among the guests, the feeling that she was being watched didn't hit her suddenly. There was no prickling at the back of her neck; no hairs rankled. Still, an undeniable awareness slowly grew within her.

Stopping, she scanned the crowd and found Michael, darling, striding purposefully, inexorably toward her.

She took an involuntary half step backward. She had thought him permanently occupied with the blonde. Now he was here, stalking her. And tonight was no time to deal with the discomfort she felt when around him.

Her silver sandals beat a tattoo on the parquet floor as she retreated toward the kitchen. But Mike headed her off near a set of French doors.

"Ellie," he said, staying her with a firm hand on her lower arm. "We haven't had a chance to talk."

"Isn't it a shame? But it's always like that at these functions." She knew her smile was bright, false. "But I hope you're enjoying yourself."

Underneath she was flustered. Her skin seemed to ripple, to tingle beneath his fingers. She steeled herself against it.

"I wanted to apologize for this afternoon," he said, "and thank you. You saved my life."

"I just happened to be there and you just happened to pull over, and..." She'd learned a long time ago the danger inherent in taking credit for something over which she had no control, even when it turned out well. She refused to accept either the danger or the credit. "I am glad you weren't hurt," she said. "But I really need to be in the kitchen, so if you'll excuse me..."

He kept his hand where it was. "What's in the kitchen you can't find out here? The tables are loaded with hors d'oeuvres."

"And I have to make certain they stay that way."

"Isn't the caterer supposed to— Oh, are you the caterer?"

"I'm the person who hired the caterer. A very temperamental man, I might add. So please—"

"Give me a minute first." He urged her toward the French doors. "Out here."

"I said I don't have time." She kept her smile but could feel its brightness fading.

"If I insist?"

"Insist and be damned," she blurted. She couldn't afford to offend any of the guests tonight, unless she absolutely had to. But Mike might prove the exception. "Even if I had time to go outside with you, it's raining out."

He released her and peered out the window. "You're right. It is." Jamming his hands into his trouser pockets, he crossed his feet. "Then we can talk right here."

"Look, my company has a lot riding on this party, and I'm going to be busy all night long making sure everything goes well."

"Won't you even take a break?"

Before she could answer, the sound of metal clattering loudly against tile exploded from the kitchen, followed by a string of French profanity. Swearing softly, Ellie rushed inside.

Mike followed.

Jean, the caterer, a small, dark-haired man, lay sprawled on the floor, cursing a blue streak in French. By his side, next to a waiter who was poised on his knees, lay two large, overturned baking trays, and hors d'oeuvres were scattered over the floor and counters. Several fish-paste puffs were stuck to the ceiling, and a couple more adhered to Jean, one dipping slightly over his left eyebrow.

As best as Ellie could decipher, Jean had tripped on a piece of cabbage or some other of *les crudités* that had been dropped on the floor.

Ignoring Mike's amusement, Ellie used her diplomatic and organizational skills to soothe Jean, then directed the cleanup and the production of fresh hors d'oeuvres.

She didn't notice when Mike left; he simply disappeared at one point or another. Perhaps he'd gone back to the blonde.

As far as she was concerned, it was the best place for him, as long as it kept him out of her way. Some strange chemistry between them—she refused to label it bad luck—proved disastrous for her practically every time he was close by.

He was dangerous and shouldn't even be allowed in public, at least not anywhere near Ellie Logan.

As the evening progressed, she had little time to think about him, though she remained aware of his whereabouts as she supervised the help in the ballroom. She called her awareness self-protection. Perhaps if she stayed as far away from him as possible she could salvage the remainder of the evening.

But matters in the kitchen deteriorated even further. Two of the waiters disappeared, wearing the tuxedos she had supplied.

Celui qui veut, peut, she reminded herself. He who will, can.

Ellie would, could. So, with champagne tray in hand, she returned to the ballroom.

Reveling in his blessed aloneness, Mike lounged in an isolated corner. He'd slipped away while Laura and Buck were dancing earlier, had visited with some of his father's old friends and some of his own business acquaintances, had even blundered upon his half brother once. David had acknowledged Mike, though not eagerly, or even politely. Whenever David spoke to

Mike, he sounded as if his mouth were full of hot rubber.

Mike wondered if David talked to everyone that way or if his tongue thickened only in the presence of his illegitimate sibling. Whichever, it didn't matter to Mike.

He had gleaned some information from Nora Chapman about Ellie as well. Not much, but more than Ellie had offered. He'd learned that her family was from El Paso—the banking Fairfields, Nora had called them. He'd heard of the family vaguely, enough to know they were wealthy. Apparently family money hadn't kept Ellie out of the marketplace, or from working for a living. Neither of the jobs he'd seen her involved in spoke of the type of society from which Nora had implied Ellie came.

"Have you been avoiding me, Michael?"

Laura's voice startled him. If he'd seen her coming, he would have evaded her. Instead he smiled slowly and asked, "Where's Buck?"

"What is it with you and my husband? If it were anyone else I'd think there was more than business going on between you. Well, business will have to wait. Someone else caught him first. Thank God." She traced the edge of Mike's satin lapel. "I wanted to see you alone again."

Stiffening, Mike retreated. He had seen this coming, had been avoiding it for the entire six months he'd done business with Morgan Oil. He had to be diplomatic; he couldn't risk compromising his business with Buck by offending Laura.

"You're such a coward," Laura said, pouting. Stalking like a predator, she regained the space he had put between them.

He sidestepped. "And you're a beautiful woman. But, Laura—"

"Don't 'but' me, darling."

"If Buck ever found out—"

"Who's going to tell him? You?" She grasped his lapels again. On the surface, he mused, she was like silk clinging to satin; underneath, like iron welded to iron. "Me?" She brought her face so close to his that her breath feathered across his mouth.

"How about them?" He gestured toward the room with a jerk of his head, then stepped backward into something soft. He swiveled toward it—swiveled toward Ellie.

She fought the tray she carried as if it were alive, obviously trying to restore her balance, but the tray toppled awkwardly, the crystal flutes tumbling to the floor, bowl over stem, splashing champagne across the skirt of Laura's dress and the front of Ellie's.

Ellie's face reflected an equal measure of horror and desperation. Mike could almost read her mind: she'd worked hard on this party, and this accident could ruin it.

He could see Laura's tantrum building by her vindictive expression. She could play hell with Ellie's career, just as she could play hell with his.

Again CinderEllie had saved him for the moment, though inadvertently. And, as before, it had been at her own expense.

Three

Monday morning, Mike scowled at his secretary from the doorway of his office. "Where'd you put that report on the Dunes well?"

Dixie scowled back. "It's on your desk, right under your nose. If it'd been a snake..." She returned to her typing. "What's eating you, anyway? Somebody steal your mud samples or something?"

Mike scraped his hand down his jaw and heaved a sigh. "I guess I'm a bit distracted lately," he admitted.

Distracted was the least of it. He was also disappointed and very nearly discouraged, all because of delightful, unpredictable CinderEllie.

She'd sneaked out on him the first time and then last Saturday treated him as if he had the plague. He didn't expect to appeal to every woman in the world, of course—he'd be tickled pink if Laura Morgan found him unattractive. But why Ellie? Why should this woman, to whom he felt so drawn, turn away from him?

"Mi-ike. Are you still with me?" When Dixie had brought him back to the here and now, she said, "Some of these investors are driving me crazy."

"Who now?"

"That fool friend of Buck Morgan's has been pestering me all week about his investment. I told him the East Texas well hasn't been operating long enough to pay off, but he won't stop calling. He's like a setting hen with only one egg on the nest. Could you switch his investment to something that'll get him off my back?"

"Even if he switches," Mike warned her, "he'll only have one egg."

"Just check, please."

Mike chuckled. "In the meantime, see if you can reach Alan Thompson for me. He's one investor I'd love to have pestering you."

Bills and receipts and time cards cluttered Ellie's desk. Across the jumble, Swan narrowed her dark eyes critically at her partner. "You look like the wrath of God. Maybe you should've stayed home."

"You're the one who had the flu. Besides," Ellie said, her voice foreboding, "when I should've stayed home was last Saturday."

Today, two days after the Regina disaster, she still felt the aftershocks of it, hadn't slept in two nights because of worrying—and looked it, she knew.

Her face was pale, hardened by the hair pulled back into its usual knot and by her charcoal-gray pin-striped suit. But the oversize tortoiseshell reading glasses did hide somewhat the blood-streaked whites of her eyes.

Swan, on the other hand, looked as striking and as elegant as always. Even the flu hadn't faded her ebony skin or dulled her almond-shaped eyes or lessened the proud angle of her chin.

"I think you should call it a learning experience," Swan said. Aside from being Ellie's partner, her friend and the most efficient person she'd ever met, Swan was masterful at pointing out the obvious.

"I did learn an invaluable lesson," Ellie agreed.

When Swan tilted her head, her chin-length black hair swung freely to the side. "From now on we're only going to use experienced waitresses?"

"*I'm* experienced; I've just been jinxed. And that's what I learned. If that man ever gets within shouting range again, he won't see me for the dust; I'll be gone quicker than a West Texas wind." She shuddered. "You can't imagine how horrible it was. I dumped champagne all over the wicked witch of Dallas!"

"Her dress cleaned up all right, didn't it?" Swan asked, as if nothing else mattered. Then she waved a stack of papers. "Are these all the bills from the florist?"

"Hmm? Yeah, that's it. And yes, Laura darling's dress cleaned up, thanks to some two-stepping we did with a bottle of club soda, and thanks to that husband of hers. Once he got there, not only did she help us, but she also calmed down. Who knows for how long? If she's not spiteful, I'm a monkey's grandmother.''

Swan snorted. "This time I'm pulling for Granny."

Ellie flipped through a stack of invoices. "I think we have everything—" A chime sounded from the front office. "Including a visitor. Joanne's not out there, is she?"

Swan stood. "I'll see who it is."

After Swan left, Ellie rummaged through her desk until she found an aspirin bottle, then downed two with water from the carafe on her cherry Queen Anne writing desk.

Their offices were like the Sunday-school dresses she'd worn as a child: all rose and gray and pretty and neat. The dresses had hidden her skinned knees and bandaged elbows; the office presented a cover for the struggles she and Swan had put into the Genies.

Outside Swan spoke in a moderated tone. Ellie detected the rise and fall of normal inflection in her partner's voice, broken by an occasional bass rumble. A disturbingly familiar rumble.

Straightening her glasses determinedly, Ellie crossed over to the door. She merely intended to check, simply meant to listen a bit to better prepare herself for whoever it might be. Never mind that she hadn't listened at a door since she was thirteen. Lately she seemed to be doing many things she'd rarely done before.

She rested her ear against the crack in the door. And she heard Swan insisting that Ellie was busy, couldn't be disturbed.

Good for Swan, she thought.

A man's voice responded, a voice that was as rich and smooth as chocolate. Sweet suffering Samuel! It was Mike what's-his-name, cajoling, charming, sweet-talking. How in blazes had he found her? And why?

Her curiosity was strong, but her survival instinct overpowered it. Ellie prayed Swan would hold her ground, since there wasn't anywhere to hide in her office.

She leaned closer to the door, cupping her ear as Swan asked Mike what he wanted. Maybe he would say, Ellie thought. Perhaps, for once when around him, she might prove fortunate. Maybe he'd satisfy her curiosity without her having to face him again.

But then again, maybe not. For some reason, Swan began to agree with him.

Ellie's astonishment slowed her reaction. She didn't realize that Swan had crossed the outer office until the door swung outward and she stumbled forward.

Awkwardly she tried to steady herself, staggering one step, two steps. Then she caught herself and pulled upright, her glasses tilting crookedly.

Mike smiled at her over Swan's shoulder. "Hello, Ellie."

Ellie nudged her glasses straight and, in the face of defeat, tentatively returned his smile.

"Mike, how surprising." She held out her hand.

He gripped it firmly, and his handshake sent vibrations to the tips of her toes. Her stomach dipped as well.

"Your secretary said you were busy." He released her hand. "But I convinced her I wouldn't keep you long."

"She's my partner," Ellie clarified. Her glance toward Swan was meant to speak volumes, but no less so than Swan's shrug.

Mike's grin was apologetic. "Sorry. I'm Mike Bannister."

"I'm Swan Stephens." Swan offered her hand. "And I'm so glad to meet you. I've heard a lot about you." She flashed a questioning glance at Ellie, then added, "I think." She wandered back to their secretary's desk and began ruffling through some papers on top—still listening, Ellie thought wryly.

"I'd like to talk with you, Ellie," Mike said. "May I come in?"

"Must you?"

"We could conduct our business in this doorway, I guess."

Behind him, Swan chuckled softly. Ellie frowned. "What business?"

Mike leaned against the door frame. "I understand you hire people out for unusual temporary jobs."

"You really want to talk business?" Ellie asked suspiciously.

He nodded.

Reluctantly she ushered him in. When he was settled, she faced him from across her desk. "Now," she said, feeling relatively secure, "what kind of job do you want done?"

Instead of answering, he stretched his legs out in front of him and crossed his feet at the ankles.

Although he was taking his time about getting to it, he looked as if he were here on business. In a navy suit, a soft-blue shirt and a striped silk tie, he had enough physical presence to orchestrate a multimillion-dollar deal.

"Your job," she prodded him. "What was it?"

"Why did you sneak out that Friday we first met?"

His question surprised her. She pulled off her glasses and leaned back in her chair. "I didn't sneak out. I . . . left."

"In that case, why did you—" he echoed her pause "—leave?"

She tapped her folded glasses against her hand. An explanation wasn't necessary, she knew, and yet she felt compelled to offer one. But not the whole truth. That would expose a vulnerability that she always kept hidden. She couldn't tell him she'd been unnerved by the attraction she'd felt for him. Even now a strange apprehension grew within her. She simply wasn't strong enough to deal with the likes of Mike Bannister.

So she told only part of the truth. "When I realized I wasn't going to clean up well enough to return to the party, there seemed no reason to stay."

"What about your shoes?"

She smiled. "I picked them up on the way out."

"In the janitor's closet that wasn't down from the telephone room."

"Did I say telephone room? My mistake. It's on the opposite side of the building." She slid her glasses back on.

Mike radiated strength and confidence; his eyes held an intensity that cut to the center of her. If ever she were ready for involvement, he would certainly make a fine candidate. But that was a big if.

"Now what is it you want from the Genies?" she asked.

"Why didn't you at least say goodbye?"

She fidgeted with a pencil on her desk. "We didn't know each other; I didn't think we'd ever meet again. Walking away seemed quicker, easier."

"And safer?"

Her mouth gaped. What was he? Some kind of mind reader?

When she didn't answer, he asked, "Did you return to your elegant party?"

"Not exactly. You did say you wanted a job done, right?"

"What about your friend's Porsche?"

"I returned it, none the worse for wear, in spite of you and the mop bucket."

"And you walked home?"

"I took a taxi."

"I would've driven you, if you'd stayed around a little longer."

She breathed in deeply, then out slowly. The man could try the patience of a saint! "Do you or do you not have a job for the Genies?"

"I do," he said. "I also have something for you." From his pocket he took Great-aunt Hilda's comb and slid it across the desk. "I can't say it's as good as new, but it's as good as I could manage to have it repaired."

She lifted the comb and studied it incredulously. "Thank you," she said, but she thought her gratitude sounded so inadequate. His thoughtfulness filled her with a rich warmth, an undeniable pleasure. "This has a great deal of sentimental value." She smiled slowly. "I do appreciate your having it repaired." She tucked the comb into her desk drawer. "Now, what can we do for you?"

"I need a temporary employee."

"That's what we're here for." Ellie pulled a form in front of her. "Tell me about the job."

"Is it true that you handle some off-the-wall requests?"

"Such as?"

"Such as, I understand you've attended certain functions with . . . a few gentlemen who needed truly socially acceptable partners."

She cupped her chin in her hand and waited.

"I heard you've handled several assignments such as that, that you're a good actress and you take some . . . well, some odd jobs. Some people might call mine odd."

"Again—odd jobs are our specialty."

"I don't think you realize how strange mine is."

"I won't unless you tell me. But keep in mind that we don't do anything illegal."

"Oh, it's not illegal." Mike rubbed his hand over his jaw.

She tossed her pencil onto the desktop. "Good. Now. What is it?"

"I need to hire some luck."

She laughed; she couldn't help it. If she offended him, she didn't care. This man, her nemesis, the man who'd convinced her she was the unluckiest thing since the *Titanic*, actually wanted to hire his luck through her.

"I'm serious," he said.

She tried to compose herself. "So am I. You obviously don't know the slightest thing about us, about me, and you want *me* to find you a bit of luck."

"Not find it," he explained. "Just rent it to me."

She cleared her throat. "What is it you want? A real genie? That's only our name; we're not magical."

"I'm not looking for a genie." He articulated slowly, as if she were hard of hearing. "Just you. I have a critical meeting on Thursday, and I want you there as my temporary luck."

"Look, I'm not lucky. I'm just plain, ordinary, get-up-in-the-morning-and-go-to-work Ellie Logan."

"You may be that to everyone else. To me you'll always be CinderEllie."

She bit back her astonishment. "That's ridiculous."

"Nevertheless." Mike held her gaze so intently that she almost squirmed under it. The man could jump-start a heartbeat. "I'm not asking for forever," he told her. "Just one meeting; a couple of hours and it'll be over."

"No," she told him. "The answer is no."

He settled further into his chair, resting his foot on his knee. "Why?"

"My business is on the up-and-up. Your request isn't."

"It is, you know. And if it would make you feel better, you could take notes at the meeting. Be a secretary. I don't care."

"I can hire a secretary for you, a good one."

"Dammit, I don't want a secretary!" He tapped his fist against his knee. "I just want you to have lunch with me and a couple of other people. One lunch, that's all. This meeting's important."

She could tell it was by the intensity of his gray eyes, by the set of his jaw, by the sobriety of his expression.

She was foolish to weaken even a little, absurd to consider his notion. Still, considering wasn't agreeing.

Mike Bannister, the man, wasn't her main reason for balking. Long ago she'd vowed never to accept responsibility for anything over which she had no control. And she would have no control whatsoever over the outcome of his meeting.

"Look at it from my point of view," he said. "I'm an independent oilman, a wildcatter. These days, that's almost insane in itself. And something out of the ordinary happens every time I run into you. Something serendipitous, too good to be true, only it is. This meeting on Thursday's important enough that I'll stack the deck any way I can. It'll only be a couple of hours," he cajoled her.

"What's so important about it?"

"It's with two potential investors, and if they choose to invest in Bannister Drilling, it'll mean more to my company than you can imagine. Not only will they bring their own funds, but their investment will encourage other investors, as well." He paused. "I'm not talking about charity. The benefit goes both ways; they'll get their money's worth."

"If you're an independent, why do you need investors?"

"That's independent as in not part of a conglomerate. I'm not independently wealthy, and the money has to come from somewhere."

She removed her glasses, folded them, then tapped them against her hand. Finally she said, "Let me think about it. Leave your number with Swan; someone will get back to you."

"When?"

"When I've made up my mind."

"I'll be in touch tomorrow." He handed her a card. "If you have any questions, call me. My office number's on the front, my home number on the back."

Ellie was on edge for the remainder of the day and on into the evening. At home that night she spent her restless energy by cleaning an already clean oven, mopping a sparkling kitchen floor and tackling every cobweb that had dared to form in the corners of her house.

Finally when everything but the walls had been washed—including Ellie herself—she slipped into satin, tailored pajamas and flicked on a late movie.

As Ginger and Fred tangoed across the screen, Ellie reviewed Mike's request. Swan had favored taking his job offer, had maintained that his was an uncomplicated, undemanding request. Simply attending a business meeting without job responsibilities might be weird, but it was easy enough. Why not humor the eccentric man?

But Ellie felt an implied sense of responsibility about the outcome of this meeting as well and any decisions Mike might make because she was present. She rejected the notion that decisions based on intuition and hunches produced success. In fact, his describing her as his temporary luck sent chills coursing through her.

Though she and Swan had been close since college, Ellie had never shared with her friend or anyone else the blame she carried. Her failure to live up to her responsibilities years ago had caused the grieving guilt that lay beneath her surface.

She'd managed to accept responsibility over the years, but only when the results were hers to bear alone. She cherished her freedom from responsibility to others and guarded it almost obsessively.

Swan was a full partner who accepted her half of the accountability for their business, an undemanding friend who expected no coddling from anyone, thereby affording Ellie that full measure of freedom.

Mature adults kept their own counsel, made decisions based on fact, depended on their inner resources and hard work to achieve success. That's how she and Swan operated. If Mike Bannister didn't, he was a fool. If he played hunches, relied on intuition and counted on luck, that was his problem, not hers.

Swan's advice, then, made sense in a way. Why not humor the guy? Soon enough he'd discover his folly. And maybe from it he would learn an expensive but valuable lesson.

Now that she'd made up her mind, Ellie felt no need to wait for tomorrow. Picking up the phone, she dialed the number Mike had written on the back of his business card.

"Okay, all right, Mr. Bannister," she said after the beep on his answering machine sounded. "One meeting; one lunch. That's all. And you pay the Genies' going rate."

Four

One meeting, one lunch. The words became a refrain that carried Ellie through the next few days, then through the lunch itself. She didn't pretend to be Mike's secretary, and as far as she knew, he offered no explanations for her appearance at the meeting.

Nothing significant occurred; no deals were made, no promises given. If she hadn't felt so vindicated, Ellie might have spared more sympathy for Mike. But she had warned him.

When he called her Friday morning and asked her to have dinner with him and the same two potential investors, she didn't gloat. She simply said, "Enough's enough. This scheme of yours is a waste of time and money."

"How do you figure that?"

"What happened yesterday, that was lucky?"

"Luck doesn't always come immediately. Sometimes it ferments for a while."

"If that's the case, then practically anyone could be responsible for yours. How do you know it's been because of me?"

A moment's silence came from the other end of the line. Ellie could almost see Mike smile. Then he said, "You're the one who cast the spell."

She groaned. "I knew that was going to haunt me. But that was two weeks ago. And nothing lucky happened that night."

"That's where you're wrong. Something lucky happened at almost the exact same moment. I just didn't find out until I got home."

"*What* happened?" she asked suspiciously.

When he told her about his Dunes well, she wanted to groan again. One time, one little coincidence, and this man had put her in the same category as Marie Lebeaux, the fabled witch of New Orleans.

"You're scared, aren't you?" he said. "Afraid you might be responsible for something good happening to someone."

"That's ridiculous."

"Prove it. Have dinner with me. If you're right and you're not lucky for me, it'll simply be a dinner. Surely you can stand eating with me one more time."

When he picked her up that evening, Ellie managed to contain her self-righteousness. The man wasn't merely eccentric; he was bordering on foolish. She hoped this dinner would prove that to him, once and for all.

As he helped her on with her cashmere stole, his fingers brushed against the soft hairs on her nape. "This...overtime...is going to cost you extra, Bannister," she warned him, but her protests referred to more than overtime.

"You already told me that. And I said I'd pay." His eyes swept away from her modified Gibson topknot down to her jewel-necked white silk shirt, slowly passed over her black silk pajama pants and settled on her sling-back sandals. Every inch that his gaze touched singed, as if she'd brushed with fire.

"It'll be worth it," he said, opening the door.

"I mean this is *really* going to cost you."

He flicked her under the chin. "I can afford it."

She walked beside him, all too aware of his presence. He was one of those rare, rugged men who wore suits comfortably. His charcoal-colored jacket fit as if it had been tailored for him.

As they approached his T-bird, he admired an azalea bush that was tucked into the angle on her property where the sidewalk met the street.

"I'm not an accomplished gardener," she said, "but every now and then something lives in spite of me."

Once they were in the car, she said, "Now what is it I'm supposed to do tonight?"

He pulled away from the curb. "Just relax. Enjoy yourself."

The Lakewood area where Ellie lived was an older section of Dallas, a bit faded, a trifle worn, yet clean and patched and mended with an occasional brightly painted house to enliven the genteel shabbiness of the neighborhood.

"What do you expect to accomplish tonight that you didn't yesterday?" she asked.

"Nothing, perhaps. Then again maybe we'll work something out." He took his eyes off the traffic for a moment. "All you need to do is enjoy yourself."

Ellie found that easy. Dinner that evening went as comfortably as had lunch the day before. Alan and Libby Thompson, the investors Mike was trying to impress, were a middle-aged couple, both attractive and extremely likable.

Alan carried the conversation throughout dinner, rambling on and on about his racehorse. Not once was business mentioned.

But, Ellie decided, poking her spoon into her spumoni, Mike had had little opportunity to talk business, though he'd politely responded to Alan's intermittent questions.

Otherwise he'd spent his time acting as if he thought Ellie was the most enchanting creature he'd ever met. His gaze lingered, caressed, seduced her. And he could instill more into a simple brush of his fingers than Lord Byron ever had into his poetry.

She pitied any woman he ever seriously turned his attention toward. *She* had to fight to keep from responding in kind, and though she knew he was acting, his reasons escaped her.

"Mariah'll win that race." Alan gestured with his espresso cup. "Or I don't belong in horse racing."

"To hear him talk," Libby said, "you'd think that horse was one of our grandchildren."

"Not at all," said Alan. "He's merely an investment."

She humphed. "One of the most insane investments you ever made in the name of Thompson Enterprises."

Alan's expression showed a bridled patience. "Mariah'll be a world-class champion one day. Wait and see. And next week he'll win his first stakes race."

"Whatever. I need to powder my nose, Ellie. Would you like to come?"

In the rest room, as Ellie lounged back on a floral chintz sofa, Libby chattered, monopolizing the conversation as naturally as Alan had during dinner. "Have you known Mike long?" she asked as she patted her hairdo into shape.

Before Ellie could answer, Libby offered, "We've known him for ten years, and we just love him. He's a sweetheart. But so's his mother. Have you met her? She's such a nice lady, in spite of everything. He resembles her more than he does his father, which is for the best, I'm sure."

Ellie had been curious about Mike, but her respect for privacy, as well as her sense of business ethics, had kept her from probing into his private life and stopped her from questioning Libby now. Still, if the woman talked, what else could Ellie do but listen?

"Of course, Lucinda spoiled David and his sister," Libby commented casually, as if Ellie surely knew all about it. "Otherwise," she added as she leaned closer to the mirror and ran the tip of a finger along the edge of her lower lip, "they wouldn't be so hateful toward their own brother. Their resentment may be understandable, but it's not Mike's fault, is it? He's as much a victim of fate as they are."

Ellie nearly choked on her anticipation. She'd played by the rules with Mike and hadn't invaded his privacy, but she'd wondered. And now Libby was going to satisfy that curiosity. Ellie waited, breath held.

"Did you see the way that maître d' looked at you? Did you know him? Well, he'd sure like to know you."

Disappointment coursed through Ellie. She didn't give a hang about how the maître d' had looked at her. But obviously what she did give a hang about would be denied her, because Libby had switched to another topic.

Almost instantly Mike sensed when the two women started back across the room. It was a warm sensation that began inside him and finally erupted into a satisfied smile.

Ellie led the way. Damn, she was lovely.

"Here they are now," Alan commented, nodding toward the women. "I timed it about right, didn't I?" As they approached the table, he said to Libby, "I told him you'd be gone around twenty minutes. It's been—" he checked his watch "—nineteen minutes and twenty-two seconds. You ladies ready to leave?"

Mike stood, picking up Ellie's stole from the back of her chair. She took it from him and wrapped it around her shoulders in what seemed like an act of defiance.

Which meant, he decided, that she felt the intensity of his attraction toward her and was fighting it, or...

He refused to consider the "or."

Outside, when Alan and Libby were ready to drive off, he said to Mike, "You know where it is? Good, we'll meet you there."

Once Mike and Ellie were in the T-bird, she asked, "Where what is?"

No matter what he told her, he knew she'd argue. But he also knew that he could convince her, given sufficient time.

"Mike, what was Alan talking about?" she prodded him.

He pulled out of the parking lot onto a dimly lighted street. "Alan's a blues fan; so am I. And there's a terrific blues place in the West End, so we're going dancing."

"We who?"

"You and I and Alan and Libby."

"You and Alan and Libby can do whatever you choose," she said, "but my term of employment's over. We agreed to dinner, nothing more."

He braked at an intersection. "How does extra compensation sound?"

"You're already paying me overtime, remember?"

"I said *extra* compensation. A good negotiator at least finds out what he—or she—stands to gain," he teased her. But a better negotiator, he thought, didn't give his opponent a chance to turn him down. He turned right, heading farther into downtown, farther away from Lakewood and Ellie's house.

"Such as?" she asked.

"Such as what other business I can bring your way. And who I can introduce you to."

"Okay." She faced him. "I'll bite. What other business can you bring my way?"

"Maybe none. But maybe I can get you together with someone like Buck Morgan."

She laughed, and, beneath the passing streetlights, her face lit up, her eyes sparkling. "You mean Buck as in I-dumped-champagne-all-over-his-wife Morgan?"

"He's a good friend of mine."

"His wife, too?"

If Mike were a conceited man, he'd think Ellie was jealous.

"I could also introduce you to Ed Davis," he said offhandedly.

"*The* Ed Davis? Of Davis Oil? How do you know him?"

He'd mentioned his father to get her reaction, and her astonishment proved her lack of knowledge about his family.

Mike shrugged, trying to appear nonchalant. "He's an oilman; so am I."

"That's as irrelevant as saying that because I run a temporary service I'm automatically big buddies with Mr. Kelly of Kelly Girl."

"Aren't you?" He drove into a parking lot at the West End Marketplace.

"Wait a minute," she said. "What are we doing here?"

She obviously hadn't paid attention to where he was taking her; now the point was moot. "We're going dancing, remember?" When she began to sputter, he

said, "Now, Ellie, if you were working as a temporary secretary somewhere and the boss needed a letter
typed at quitting time, you'd finish it. We both know
that's true."

"But that's entirely different."

"No, it's not. Think of this 'assignment' as typing
a couple of letters in a different way and then I'll take
you home."

She stared intently at him for a moment, and he
could see the fires building in her eyes. Then she
sighed, and the fires seemed to fizzle. "All right," she
said. "Okay. You win."

The West End Marketplace covered several blocks
of restored warehouses adjacent to the heart of
downtown Dallas. Its brick streets and sidewalks were
lined with restaurants and clubs that attracted night-
life crowds to an otherwise sleeping city.

When Mike pushed open the door to Charlie's, the
atmosphere rolled out to greet them. A gray-haired
black man played an upright piano and sang along in
a deep voice with a melancholy tone. He teased the
keys and made the piano moan with melody while
several couples danced on the small dance floor.

After Mike and Ellie joined the Thompsons at a
corner table, they listened to the music silently for a
while. The piano player swayed on the stool, to and
fro, to the rhythm of his sad, raggy tune. He played a
few soulful chords, then he began to sing again.

Alan sipped from a glass of bourbon. "How long
ago did you go public with your stock?" he asked
Mike almost lazily, as if speaking in tune to the music
wafting around him.

Lunch yesterday and dinner tonight had all been leading to this, the moment Mike had anticipated...and dreaded. Now he needed to dust off Bannister Drilling and present the company in its Sunday best.

"About three years ago," he said. "At the time, I needed capital badly, and my chances of raising it otherwise were slim."

He didn't mention his father or his father's money or his father's company. Alan knew that situation as well as did most businessmen in Dallas.

"As it turned out," Mike went on, "I never worked so hard in all my life. I had to convince investors they could get in on the ground floor of a company that was about to become really big."

Alan sipped his drink. "I understand your stock is now widely held."

Mike nodded.

"But you still have a need for private investors?"

"With the cost of equipment today, the need's paramount." Mike smiled. "You know that, of course. The time's past when someone, like my grandfather, could start out with a notebook and a few leases and make a fortune. Today either a man's part of a conglomerate or he scrabbles."

Alan chuckled. "Scrabbling sounds like something my daddy did. As a matter of fact, Libby and I scrabbled a day or two when we were younger."

"I don't know about you two," Libby said, "but I'm glad my scrabbling days are done."

"Don't rest on your laurels, Libby girl," Alan warned her. "We could be scrabbling again quicker than you can say 'Here comes Arabian oil.'"

After that, the tenor of the conversation changed. Sooner or later, Mike knew, the Thompsons would decide. And tonight seemed to put them one step closer to a decision in his favor.

Later, when he took Ellie into his arms on the dance floor, she stiffened. In focusing his attention on Alan earlier, he'd lost sight of the fact that Ellie was here as an employee, as his bought-and-paid-for lucky charm. The memory now brought him little pleasure. He wanted to forget their business relationship, wanted to enjoy the pleasure he felt in being around her.

So he tugged her closer and whispered, "Remember, we're just typing."

By the end of the second song, she began to relax. But the more she eased in his arms, the more tense his own body felt.

Two weeks had passed since he'd first laid eyes on her, and during that time he'd been tantalized by the question of how it would feel to hold her in his arms. Now he knew.

Silently he began to recite the presidents of the United States. As a child, he'd used this technique when he'd needed to hide his emotions, and usually by the time he hit Lincoln, the monotonous recitation calmed him. Now he'd already reached Chester Arthur, and he still felt fire in his blood. He closed his eyes.

After a few moments, he felt Ellie pull back, slightly, then lean forward as if she were peering over his shoulder.

He opened his eyes. "What are you doing?"

"Wondering who's navigating. Your eyes were closed," she accused him.

He pulled her close again. "I wouldn't steer you wrong; I've got this dance floor memorized."

"Are you tired? Shall we go back to the table?"

"I'm fine. Don't you ever stop talking?" he asked. "I thought you were finally relaxed."

"I was until I realized no one's at the wheel." Apparently satisfied now, she danced silently in his arms for a moment. Then she asked, "How long have Alan and Libby been married?"

"They aren't. They were once—actually twice—but they aren't anymore." He rubbed his chin against her hair. "Alan is married to someone else now, someone younger, and Libby's dating someone younger as well. This is a business dinner," he explained further. "And Libby and Alan are business partners."

"But they seem to like each other so much."

"I guess they both just needed someone more exciting."

"What's so exciting about young?"

He arched an eyebrow. "You should know, my child," he teased her.

"Twenty-seven's hardly a child."

"That depends on one's perspective. Alan's someone younger is forty-two; Libby's is thirty-five."

"Oh—" Ellie grinned impishly. "Good for Libby." After another half circle of the dance floor, she asked, "Have you ever been married?"

"Nope. How about you?"

"Me neither. You think there might be something wrong with us?"

"Nothing at all, aside from our being sane in an insane world."

"You consider marriage an insanity?"

Mike shrugged. Though marriage itself hadn't been the problem with his parents, it had certainly caused the problem.

But tonight he didn't want to delve into those old memories. So he said a trifle cavalierly, "I've seen people miserable in marriage and outside of it. If I'm going to be miserable, I'd rather be by myself."

"You don't seem to be the miserable type—"

He chuckled. "See? It works."

The pianist had played without pause for a while, segueing from one blues tune to another. Now, after a crescendo of chords, the music stopped.

When they returned to the table, Libby said, "You two dance so well together it reminds me of when Alan and I were dating."

"Which time?" Alan asked.

"Certainly not the first. You were too awkward back then."

"Every kid's awkward in his teens, darlin'."

Libby rolled her eyes. "You were twenty-one."

Alan chuckled. "Well, I'm not anymore. And neither are you. You ready to go?"

"Already?" Mike said.

"My wife gets cranky if Libby keeps me out too late. Unreasonable of her, I know, but what can I say? That doesn't mean you two have to go."

"Oh, but it does," Ellie said, rising. She smiled at Mike, placed a hand on his shoulder and murmured softly, "I've finished my typing."

The drive from downtown to Lakewood was short, and never had Ellie appreciated that as little as she did tonight. In spite of her reservations, she'd enjoyed the evening. For the first time, nothing embarrassing, or unlucky had happened to her in Mike's presence.

And nothing lucky had happened to him. Maybe now he'd accept that she was no more a lucky charm for him than he was a jinx to her.

Strangely enough, she didn't feel as justified as she should. Probably because she was tired, she thought.

But this kind of tired she'd order refills of if she could. She wasn't sleepy, despite the drowsing clack of the windshield wipers Mike turned on against the sudden rain. Her heart pumped rapidly, zinging blood through her veins. She felt invigorated, alive down to the silk-stockinged toes in her strappy sandals.

After parking in front of her house, Mike said, "It's been a marvelous evening, Ellie. Thank you."

She breathed deeply, then, almost awkwardly, said, "Well, see you around."

"Wait." He stilled her with a hand on her arm. "Give me a minute, please."

That minute was fraught with a stomach-clenching tension. There was no one else around now, and Mike was still acting intrigued by her. And the idea that it might not be an act disturbed her. She wasn't sure she knew how to deal with the change in their relationship.

Finally she said, "Well," and her voice cracked like a pubescent boy. She tried again. "Well, you really didn't accomplish what you set out to achieve."

"I didn't?"

"Nothing lucky happened."

"I think it did. On the other hand, nothing unlucky happened to you."

"Amazing, isn't it?"

"Yes," he said huskily, "it is." With his hand on her arm, he began pulling her slowly toward him.

His touch quickened her blood. Her senses seemed suddenly sharpened, her clothing almost intrusive on her skin, the silk harsh across her nipples.

Still, she moved into his arms willingly. His embrace seemed as inevitable—and as desirable—as the coming of spring. For one moment she would allow herself to take what he had to offer. For just a moment.

He framed her face with his hands. Gently, deliberately, he brushed a knuckle down her nose, then back and forth across her mouth.

Her body liquefied under his touch, heated unbearably as his head dipped and his lips covered hers, firm and demanding.

She met that demand eagerly, giving back all that she took, moving her mouth sensuously under his. And his caress grew around her, enveloping her in a gentle, persuasive aggression.

She knew she couldn't allow the embrace to last much longer, knew that she would have to end it soon. But not yet.

He slid his tongue between her lips in a sensual invasion, and she gasped as a delicious sensation flowed through her. Then Mike shaped his hands around her head and held her tighter still, until their bodies were almost one. She felt the throb of his heartbeat against her, the thrill of his muscles against her softness. Never had a first kiss felt so right to her, so natural, yet so exciting.

Then he withdrew, lifting his mouth only. "Ahh Ellie," he sighed, his breath warm against her mouth. He curled his knuckles into the hollow of her neck.

It took every bit of strength she possessed to break the contact. "I really do need to go in," she said shakily.

He nodded, reluctantly releasing her.

Her knees felt wobbly as Mike helped her out of the car. When she stepped under the umbrella he held for her, she looked up into his gray eyes, and the sole of her sandal slipped, skidding off the wet curb. She grabbed at him, clutching his sleeve as she fell into the azalea bush.

"Oh, no," she wailed. "It's broken."

Mike bent over her, obviously trying to cradle her in his arms. "What's broken?" he breathed, his voice full of anxiety.

"Ouch." She swore uncharacteristically and shifted her weight to one hip. She groaned.

"Don't move, Ellie." He patted her ineffectually. "I'll call the paramedics."

She plucked at a sharp twig that was stabbing her ribs, then yanked at another that was tangled in her hair, poking her scalp. Then what he'd said registered.

"Paramedics? For my azalea?"

He straightened, his face a study in disbelief. "Your *azalea's* broken?"

"I wouldn't be this upset if it were my ankle."

Her ankle *was* throbbing, and her shin stung. When she lifted her foot and began massaging the ankle, her sandal hung from her toes. The broken strap dangled; her ripped stocking laddered up her ankle.

"Are you sure you're not hurt?" Mike folded an arm around her.

She restrained her growl, barely, and replanted her foot, this time more solidly. Then she picked up a broken branch and scowled. "Look at this."

Mike swallowed. "I see it."

The son of a sea turtle was laughing! He was biting it back, sure, but behind that swallow had been laughter, pure and simple.

"What's so funny?" she demanded. "Share the joke, please."

"No joke. I just think you're wonderful." He took the branch from her. "And so's your azalea. Come on. Let's get some ice on that ankle."

Exasperated, she limped toward the door. "I don't need a nurse, thank you. Besides," she muttered, "the way things are going I'd probably slip on the ice and break my neck." At the door, she said a firm goodnight and left him on the porch.

Although Ellie didn't believe in charms or lucky pieces or jinxes, the next morning she was still trying to convince herself that she'd fallen into the azalea bush accidentally. Mike could no more be a jinx for her than she could be a charm for him, she reassured herself as she matched the day's jobs to her available employees.

In midmorning Joanne, the secretary she and Swan shared, put a call through to her.

"Ms. Logan," Ellie announced.

"How's your ankle?"

She recognized his distinctive voice—husky yet smooth—and her spirits lifted, inexplicably, maddeningly.

"My ankle and my shin are sore, thank you," she replied, exasperated that the sound of his voice could affect her mood so strongly. "About what you'd expect after being tackled by an azalea."

"In that case, how about having lunch with me?"

She twirled the telephone cord around her fingers. "Is this invitation for Ellie, the good luck charm?" she asked skeptically.

"Would you say yes?"

"No."

"Then how about just plain Ellie Logan?"

Why not? she thought. Why the heck not? "That Ellie," she said, "would love to."

They met at a Chinese restaurant two blocks from her office. The mere sight of Mike brought back all the feelings his kiss had forged in her, and as she dwelled on that unnerving memory, her heart faltered and her breath clogged in her chest.

So she played with her almond chicken and tried to keep her mind on answering his questions about her business.

"My most unusual job? Mostly," she said, "we do ordinary things. Shop for a birthday present for a busy executive's wife or sometimes serve breakfast in bed for a special occasion." She forked a chunk of chicken and studied it. "I guess my most unusual job was when I delivered a bottle of wine to Joel Howard's hotel room."

"The millionaire?"

She nodded. "He's a busy man and wouldn't see just anyone. My client wanted to get his attention, to sell him on using Texas wine in his exclusive restaurants." She shrugged. "So I dressed up like Emmett Kelly and hid inside a room-service cart."

Mike laughed. "Did he buy the wine?"

"Not exactly," she admitted. Then she grinned. "But I got his attention."

He cocked his head. "Were you ever embarrassed by what you had to do on any of your jobs?"

"You mean like hiding in the cart?" She shook her head. "I'm not an introvert. In fact, I once dreamed of being an actress. So this is a perfect job for me. What about you? Does wildcatting suit you?"

"I can't imagine doing anything else, even with the mess the industry's in."

"Has the oil slump affected you badly?"

"Not until recently. My father saw what was happening long ago and helped me prepare for it, so I've been able to hang in there when many independents have failed." He smiled wryly. "When my father talks oil, people listen."

"He's an oilman?"

"He and my grandfather and my brother, too."

"What about your sister?"

He frowned. "Who told you about Sarah?"

To alleviate the suspicion Ellie read in his eyes, she said, "Libby Thompson mentioned her."

After a moment he said, "If you call living off the profits being in oil, then I guess Sarah is. You might say we're an oil family. Sort of the way your family's in banking."

"And who's been talking about me?"

"Nora Chapman said she's known your grandparents for a long time. I gather she felt a bit uncomfortable that you were an employee at her party, instead of a guest."

"That's why I try to avoid working for friends," Ellie said.

He clasped his teacup in both hands and studied her over the top of it. "Does that mean I can't be your friend and your client, too?"

She didn't like the tone of his voice; he sounded the way he had twice before when he'd hired her as his lucky charm. She was fed up with being used as a rabbit's foot. "If I said yes?"

"That would make things difficult, because I have another job for you."

She pushed her plate away. "What kind?"

"I only need you for one day," he told her. "One normal, eight-hour work day."

"As a typist or receptionist?"

"Not exactly. I want you to come with me to Hot Springs for Mariah's big race." He swirled his teacup. "Alan and Libby would like for you to come, too."

She sighed. "Mike, you're wasting your money trying to hire a good-luck piece."

"I promise, this job'll be no more unusual than a shopping trip, or serving someone breakfast in bed."

"There is a matter of some three hundred miles between here and Hot Springs."

"That's no problem. We'll be flying in a private plane. Wouldn't you like to see the races?" he teased her.

She was tempted. She'd never been to the races and had always wondered about its attraction. Besides, how many times did she get a job offer that combined business and pleasure so...agreeably?

Before she'd even consider it, though, one thing needed to be clarified.

"I'm not saying I'll go, but if I do, who's the pilot?"

"Don't worry. Alan's flying us. We'll be taking the Thompsons' company plane."

She drummed her fingers on the tabletop. Should she risk it? she wondered. On the one hand, he'd made a valid job offer. And she was in the business of staying in business.

On the flip side lurked her undeniable attraction to him. She was beginning to truly like Mike, and she enjoyed his company immensely. Did she dare risk life and limb and Heaven knew what else for the sake of that?

"You're talking about one more day and that's all. Right?" She narrowed her eyes. "Then I'll think about it. Just think—that's all I'm promising."

Five

From the moment they landed in Hot Springs, Ellie's excitement escalated. Although she'd watched horse racing on television and seen it in the movies, she'd never before felt this sense of eagerness and breathless anticipation.

The golden rays of the Arkansas sun spilled over the Thompsons' private box like treasure from a chest. The railing barely held back Alan, Libby and all their enthusiasm, but Mike maintained his easygoing air, with his feet lazily propped on the railing.

"Come on, Daylight. Move it!" Holding his binoculars up to his eyes, Alan urged a trailing bay stallion around the track.

Libby cheered for a different horse. "Come on, Dover," she called. "Come on."

The horses pounded by.

"Get the lead out, Daylight," Alan yelled.

"Move it, Dover," cried Libby.

Ellie's pulse rushed, and she could feel the flush rise in her face. For the first time in her life she understood the magnetism racing could hold.

"And it's Trifle across the finish line by a head," said the announcer, "followed by Wanderlust, with Welfare in third. Daylight's fourth and Dover fifth. Here comes..."

"Fourth," Alan exploded. "That blasted sack of hay came in fourth!"

"Your sack of hay beat mine," Libby laughed. "I sure hope we made a better choice with Mariah."

"Has everyone placed their bets?" Alan asked. "Ellie? Mike?"

"I really don't care to gamble," Ellie said, tempering her words with a slight smile. "I'm just happy watching."

"Darlin', it's not gambling unless you stand a chance of losing. And Mariah's a certainty."

How many times had she heard that when she was young? Though her father's weakness had been the stock market, he'd used the same excuses, the same justifications, as gamblers everywhere. And after her mother's death, his certainties had often become disasters.

"We still have a little time," Mike said. "But we'll do it now, won't we, Ellie?"

He seemed so determined that when he urged her up, Ellie went with him, silently, until they were out of hearing range. But before he started down the aisle, she stopped. "I'll just wait here. If you want to bet on the race, go ahead, but I really don't gamble."

Impelled by his intent scrutiny, she tried to explain. "My father lost a great deal of money in the stock market. He invested as compulsively as any gambler."

"But this isn't compulsive, Ellie," Mike said. "It's a calculated risk." He grinned boyishly. "I don't invest excessively, and I don't gamble excessively, either. Still...you can stay here if you want, or you can keep me company while I take a calculated risk that Mariah'll win."

"I'll wait right here." She sat down in the grandstands.

"Okay, but if you change your mind, just whistle—I forgot. You can't, can you?"

She propped her foot on the row in front of her. "I won't need to; I'm not changing my mind."

"I'll teach you to whistle one of these days, anyway," he said with a pat on her shoulder.

As he left, another race began. The horses left the starting gate with a rush, and the crowd roared, cheering the animals on. "Come on, Calliope," came from Ellie's left. Behind her, "Go get 'em, Daisy Mae!" Again she felt the stir of the crowd's fever, the excitement of the gamble.

Calculated risk, my great-aunt Hilda, Ellie thought. As far as she was concerned, gambling was gambling. Whether it was done at a race track or in a casino or on Wall Street, the same behavior drove it.

She'd left the compulsiveness behind and avoided it since her father's death. It was one part of her father's world that she didn't miss at all.

Later, after they returned to the box, Alan could hardly sit still, waiting for Mariah's race. He kept beating the rail with a rolled-up racing form. "He's going to show them. You just wait. Mariah'll make me proud."

"Settle down, Alan," Libby said. "You're making *me* nervous."

He paid no attention to her. Instead he began to pace. "I ought to be in the back with him."

"Bailey told you to stay away," said Libby. "And you're paying him good money to train Mariah, so listen to him."

"That's right. *I'm* paying him. That makes me the boss. And I should be back there, shouldn't I?" he asked Mike.

"It's too late to worry about it," Mike told him. "They're lining up at the starting gate now."

Alan whirled back to the rail. "Omigosh," he whispered. "It's time. Come on, babe. Do it for Papa."

Mike laced his fingers through Ellie's and placed their hands in his lap. This was the only tension he showed, but still she felt it in the pressure of his fingers on hers. Could he possibly believe that his Thompson Enterprises investment depended on Mariah's success?

She returned his grip and for the first time hoped she might actually bring him luck. For the first time she *wanted* to be his good-luck charm.

"They're off," called the announcer. "And it's Cherry Pie in the lead."

With his binoculars practically glued to his eyes, Alan crooned to the horse. "Give it to Papa. Win this race for me, babe. Come on, come on."

"Cherry Pie's holding the lead, with Squelch moving up on the inside. Here comes Mariah, pulling up on Squelch...."

Now Alan and Libby were practically hanging over the rail. So were Mike and Ellie.

"Come on, Mariah," Libby cried.

"That's the way to do it." Mike still gripped Ellie's hand, his fingers biting into hers.

Her heart beat in rhythm with the hooves of the horses as they raced past the box.

Mariah began moving up on the other horses, came neck and neck with Squelch in second place. Ellie felt as if her chest had been squeezed; her breathing faltered.

Then Mariah passed Squelch, drew head to flank with Cherry Pie, and his long legs flew around the track. Finally he took the lead.

As the heat neared the end, the furor in the Thompsons' box rose to a frenzy. Ellie's excitement flared as brightly as everyone else's did.

"Archangel's coming up from the rear, folks," the announcer reported. "He's moving up on Cherry Pie. Now he's passed her, coming up to Squelch."

Archangel seemed to burst forth, as if he'd been held back until now. With track-eating strides, the thoroughbred closed in on Squelch, then pulled past.

The crowd's roar drowned out the voice of the announcer.

Mariah still held the lead, but barely. In the last furlong of the race, Archangel's nose was even with Mariah's flank. Then they were neck and neck and, as they crossed the finish line, nose and nose.

"It's a photo finish," cried the announcer.

Alan swore. "Mariah won by a handsbreadth. Any fool could see that."

It had looked that way to Ellie, too. She held her breath for the seconds it took before the results showed on the tote board. Then the starch drained out of her, her shoulders slumping. She'd failed.

Mariah had placed; Archangel had won.

At three o'clock the next morning, Ellie pulled another load of laundry from the dryer.

After the first shock yesterday afternoon, Alan hadn't seemed overly depressed, insisting that Mariah had done well for his first stakes race. He didn't appear to waver in the least in his claim that Mariah was world-class champion material.

Aside from the way Ellie had interpreted his grip on her hand, Mike hadn't shown any tension, either. He seemed no more disappointed in Ellie than Alan was in Mariah. Still she felt annoyed, as if she hadn't done the job for which she'd been paid.

She slapped a folded towel onto a stack of others atop the dryer. She knew she wasn't to blame for Mariah's losing the race. She would be a fool to take responsibility for something like that.

She'd considered the ins and outs of Mike's job before she'd taken it, and the reasons that had allowed her to accept it then still stood: it was his decision, his responsibility. She hadn't agreed with his reasoning, so she didn't have to carry the blame when his logic proved unsound.

So why did she feel as if she'd been tried and found wanting?

"Because you're becoming involved, dammit!" She swept her arm against all the stacks atop the dryer, sending towels and washcloths and panties and slips flying. Then she breathed in and dispassionately surveyed the tumbled laundry.

Long ago, she'd learned that she could handle responsibility only for herself. Long ago, she'd realized that she could deal with only impersonal responsibility where others were concerned, such as her employees and her clients.

She should have had more sense than to take a job like Mike's, one that involved such a nebulous kind of accountability. Her life had been fine before he had waltzed into it. She'd accepted her shortcomings and what she could and couldn't handle.

She wanted that freedom back. And, God help her, she'd have it one way or another.

Sunday, Monday and Tuesday dragged for Ellie, though business picked up. Spring fever seemed to have hit Dallas, with temperatures soaring into the seventies and smiles splitting winter-paled faces.

Monday afternoon, Ellie worked as a mime, handing out balloons at a supermarket opening. All the shoppers seemed to have an added bounce in their steps, and the children to whom Ellie gave the balloons overflowed with enthusiasm.

But some of Ellie's usual excitement was missing. Her audience still laughed in the right places, and the laughter still spurred her on. But this time she felt a flatness within herself that she'd never felt before.

Life goes on, she reminded herself over and over again. And her life would be full and rich once more, full and rich and undemanding.

She could have it all, without Mike. And she would...soon.

By Wednesday afternoon, she'd begun clock-watching, something else she'd never done before, or at least not since she and Swan had opened the Genies. But it wasn't quitting time she waited for; the hours she spent at home were no more interesting than those spent at the office.

When the phone rang early Thursday morning, everything shifted into focus with the sound of Mike's voice. "Full and rich" suddenly had a meaning.

"Remember our negotiations?" he asked. "When I said I might get you teamed up with Buck Morgan? Well, he wants to talk with you about a job, wants to see you this morning."

She was stunned. "Does he remember me?" She fiddled with the telephone cord. "I mean does he know I'm the one with the champagne?" She paused. "You know what I mean."

"He remembers, and yes, he knows. He'd still like to talk to you."

Well, she thought, it wasn't another job *for* Mike.
She wasn't breaking any resolutions in agreeing to see
Buck.

This was genuinely business.

Buck Morgan was a gracious man, and his company, Combined Enterprises, did need a temporary.
Buck obviously was not dreaming up a job at Mike's
request, as Ellie had wondered at one point.

And his job provided a new opportunity for the
Genies. They'd never supplied an executive secretary
before. Normally companies filled those jobs from
within. But Buck's situation wasn't normal. Because
of some critical negotiations he was involved in, he
needed a breathing business machine: someone who
was skilled and intelligent but lacked a knowledge of
the intricacies of his company, someone who per-
formed expertly but without questions.

Filling this type of a position satisfactorily could
lead to a number of new accounts. Could the Genies
do it? Buck had asked.

Try to stop us, Ellie swore inwardly.

That evening, while Ellie watched the ten o'clock
news in her pajamas, the doorbell rang. She slipped on
a navy satin robe, then tied the belt as she peered
through the peephole in the front door.

Mike Bannister stood on her doorstep, his suit
jacket flung over a shoulder, his shirt rumpled, his
collar open and his tie hanging halfway down his
chest.

Before she had time to even wonder why he was there, her blood sang in her veins. Why wasn't important. He *was* there, right or wrong, good or bad. And, blast his hide, she was glad to see him.

She swung the door open.

"You think you could give me a drink?" he asked.

"Come in," she said, stepping back. "You look exhausted. Is something wrong?"

"Not at all." Stepping in, he handed her a flower. "I hope your neighbor's not as crazy about his daffodils as you are about your azaleas."

"You picked this next door?"

"I left five dollars under a rock on his porch. You think he'll mind?"

"I doubt he'll even notice one's missing." She closed the door, then waved him into the living room. "Sit down," she said, "and I'll fix you a drink. What'll it be?"

He stopped her, his hand on her arm. "I did it," he said.

"Good. I'm glad." She frowned. "Did what?"

"I got that investment from the Thompsons. Finally."

"Great!" Throwing her arms around him, she hugged him exuberantly. When he pulled her tightly to him, her heart stopped. For a moment, she could have sworn the whole world stopped.

She sucked in a sharp breath and stepped away. "Well..." She faltered. "That—" she grasped her throat as if she could force the words out more strongly "—that surely calls for champagne."

By the time she returned with their drinks and the daffodil in a bud vase, Ellie was more composed.

Mike sat at the end of the leather sofa. Dressed casually in lightweight cords, he fit into her living room uniquely. His ruggedness seemed to enhance whatever it touched rather than clash with it.

In front of the sofa stood a graceful table, and on it was displayed a Lalique vase. Mike, though, appeared more interested in another vase on the end table. "It's intriguing," he said as he lifted the piece and examined its green and crystal stylized shape.

"It comes from a small town east of El Paso," Ellie told him. "From a glass factory called Texas Crystal." She began moving paperweights on a bookcase shelf next to the fireplace to make a place for the bud vase. "My father bought stock in the company a long time ago," she said as she rearranged the glass globes. "One of the few bad investments he made while my mother was alive." Her hands stilled for a moment, and she smiled. "It wouldn't be such a bad investment today."

"How's that?"

She set the daffodil in the place of honor she'd made for it. "Oh, the company brought in a CEO from the east five years ago. I met him once; he seems formidable. And he's really begun to shake the place up." She stepped away from the bookcase. "If anyone can make them profitable, I believe he can."

Mike studied her over the top of the vase, and his nostrils flared with the strength of the breath he took. In the spell of his gaze, she felt as a small animal might when backed into a corner. She didn't like the sensation; she hadn't experienced this kind of vulnerability in years.

Then the moment was gone. He replaced the vase and stretched his legs out in front of him. And she was Ellie again, not a rabbit or a squirrel but a grown woman with all her personal strengths and weaknesses.

"You look tired," she said.

"I am, a bit." He patted the sofa next to him. "Join me?"

Despite all the reasons why she shouldn't, despite her sense of helplessness a moment ago, Ellie sat on the cushion next to him as he poured the champagne. "I have something to celebrate, too," she ventured.

"The job with Buck?"

His pleasure seemed more intense for her success than for his own.

"That's great," he said.

She lifted her champagne flute. "A toast," she said, "to good deals and great people."

He clicked his glass to hers. "To ever better deals . . . and great people."

For a moment, memories teased Ellie: Mike's kiss and the strength of his body when she hugged him earlier—she couldn't stop thinking of either.

But his thoughts seemed to be elsewhere. "What did Libby tell you about my family the other day?" he asked.

She shrugged. "She said your mother was a very nice lady, and you're more like her than you are your father. Isn't your father nice?"

"That depends on who you ask."

"And if I ask you?"

"I'm prejudiced; I think he is. But I haven't always, and I suppose his reputation says he's not." He paused, then said, "My father is Ed Davis."

Ellie's mouth gaped. No wonder he'd felt so free to tease her with Davis's business!

"But," she stammered, "your name—"

"Is the same as my mother's. They're not married; I'm illegitimate."

"Oh, my stars . . . Mike, I'm sorry."

"Hey—" he grinned "—illegitimate means they've never been married. I've had lots of time to get used to it."

He might have had time, but she was certain she could still see, behind his grin, a shadow of pain in his gray eyes. How could there not be? she wondered.

"Your sister and brother . . . are they . . . ?"

"Disgustingly legitimate." Now his grin twisted ruefully. "Most of the time they're disgustingly self-righteous, too. What about your family? You're from El Paso, aren't you? Does your family live there?"

Her fingers tightened on the stem of the champagne flute. He'd exposed his past, so now it was her turn. She glanced away and shrugged, forcing a light tone. "My grandparents live there. And I have two maiden aunts who live at home. One's your typical spinster; the other . . . well, Aunt Edith's rather out of kilter for our family. Outrageous, flamboyant . . . and perfectly lovely. She's the last thing you'd expect from an old maid."

"What about your mother and father?"

She felt her smile flatten. "They're both dead."

He touched her cheek. "What happened?"

"My mother was killed in a boating accident when I was eleven. And Daddy was diabetic; when I was thirteen he died from an insulin reaction." It was an explanation she'd made dozens of times. So why was it suddenly so hard again?

"Oh, Ellie..." he said, and everything about Mike tugged at her, drawing her into the warmth of his sympathy. *You can talk to me,* the darkening of his gray eyes assured her. *I'll listen; I'll understand; I'll give ease,* he told her silently, with the touch of his knee against hers.

She looked away, moved her knee. He couldn't understand, couldn't ease. No one could. Not if they knew the whole truth.

"After that," she said, "I lived with my grandparents and Aunt Julia and Aunt Edith." She put her empty champagne flute on the coffee table. "You're lucky to still have everyone: your parents, your sister, your brother. You're a rich man."

"I guess it's all relative... and don't you dare play off that word."

His teasing lightened the atmosphere, and she giggled, more from relief than anything else.

He set his glass beside hers and stretched an arm along the back of the sofa. "Whatever gave you the idea to start a company like the Genies?"

"It just seemed to happen. I had this friend, a businessman, who needed something done, something out of the ordinary range of temporary services. And he had nowhere to turn."

"What did he want done?"

"We-ell, he was trying to make a point at a city-council meeting and wanted something unusual delivered during the session."

He began toying with the collar of her pajamas. "What exactly?"

"Actually it was a load of manure."

He guffawed, threw back his head and released a shout of laughter that vibrated throughout the room.

"There've been fortunes made from nastier jobs," she said defensively.

"I'm not laughing at you, darling," he soothed her. And as if he were comforting her, he deserted her collar, moved on to her neck.

She swallowed. "I, uh, made the delivery. And Howard made his point. So I decided there was a place for a company that would provide unusual services."

He stroked the sensitive skin of her nape, and her throat constricted.

"What do you think? You think it's a good idea? Well, I guess it doesn't matter, really. We're making it work, and that's what counts. Of course, it could be more profitable—I wish it were—but we've made it past the point where most new businesses fail," she babbled on. "And that's a feat in itself."

He put a finger over her mouth. "Ellie," he said. The huskiness in his voice made her name sound as if it were an enchantment, promising magic and mystical wonders.

He bent his head, and the distance between them vanished. His mouth, hard and firm, covered hers, soft and yielding, and she dissolved, her muscles becoming fluid and malleable, her bones pliant and unstable.

Now she knew that she wasn't the sorcerer; he was. She was the bewitched, rather than the bewitcher.

For a moment, she allowed herself the weakness of his magic, allowed herself to give in to his sorcery. For one enchanting, mesmeric moment, she returned his kiss. A tremor ran through her, and a wave of pleasure swept over her as her nipples tautened and her body came alive.

Then, with almost a superhuman effort, she pulled away.

"I'm sorry," she said. "I shouldn't have—"

He stroked his finger across her lower lip. "Why not?"

"Well, I..." She scooted away from him. She didn't want to make a big deal of it, but the more distance she could put between them, the better she'd feel. "I like you, Mike, and I'm attracted to you. But...you're my client."

"Right now I'd rather forget that. I like you, too—a lot."

She fiddled with the lapels of her robe. "Even so—"

"And that's a beginning," he said. "The beginning of a special friendship. So was our kiss. But that's all it was, Ellie. Just a kiss."

She scowled doubtfully at him, wondering if she had really come as close to losing control as she'd felt. Perhaps he was right; maybe it had been merely a kiss.

"Relax," he said, taking her hand.

"You know what I like about you?" he asked playfully. "I like the way you laugh at things that other people whine about. I've never seen anything get you down. The night I dumped the mop water on you, you came up smiling. I like that."

"Somehow, laughing's easy around you."

"Lots of people don't think so." He stroked the length of her fingers. "You're so comfortable to be with. I feel so much at ease with you. And I like the way you're real, not the least bit fake."

His praise disconcerted her. She knew she was all the things he said, sort of, but she never really looked at them as being remarkable. And there was so much more about her that he didn't know, so much that wasn't the least bit admirable.

"So we're friends," he said. "Right?"

She nodded.

"Then tell me what you like about me."

"I already did. I told you laughing's easy when we're together."

"That's all you like?"

"We-ell. I also like the way your hair curls over your forehead." She pulled a curl straight, then let it go. It bounced back into a separate ringlet.

"And I like the way I am when I'm with you; everything seems possible, easy almost. And I like your persistence, too," she said. "Some of the time."

"That's better than none of the time." He dropped a playful kiss on her mouth.

His touch scorched her. A shallow breath fluttered in her throat. "That," she said, "just crossed the friendship boundary."

"No, it didn't. Friends kiss, lots of times."

She swallowed and forced a soft chuckle. "Somehow when we kiss I forget we're friends."

"Don't," he told her, his voice sober. "I intend to kiss you as often as possible, but don't ever forget we're friends, Ellie. I won't."

His expression declared his intention as he drew toward her. He moved slowly; she had time to stop him. But she didn't. She couldn't.

He crushed his mouth against hers, overwhelming her senses even as she tried to retain some control over them.

His tongue teased, invaded, advanced, then retreated. He groaned, sliding his hands down to her waist.

Shivering with the excitement that coursed through her, Ellie yielded to his heated challenge. For this moment, her world held only Mike, his embrace and the hunger it stirred within her.

He explored the warmth of her mouth with his tongue, dipping into the intimate interior. His lips moved on hers in an electric contact that denied any attempt at retreat on her part.

She was somewhat shocked by the strength of her response and the level of her desire. Mike cupped her breast, and she knew she had to rally her defenses...now.

She withdrew, a matter of bare inches, and cleared her throat.

As if he didn't realize she was trying to put space between them, he nipped at her ear, then her neck, then gradually worked his way around her jawline and went back to her mouth.

Her knees turned to mush. Again she cleared her throat. "Mike?"

"Hmm?"

"I think we're past the parameters of friendship."

"Think so?"

He hadn't moved away, and the breath behind his words tickled her chin.

She put some more distance between them, moving to the end of the couch. "I'm convinced of it."

He lounged nonchalantly against the sofa back and wiggled his eyebrows comically. "You wouldn't consider setting some new boundaries, would you? No, I didn't think so. Looks like it's time for me to say goodnight, then."

At the door, he held her in a loose embrace. "One question," he said, "and then I'm gone." He rested his forehead against hers and, nose to nose, asked, "Were you just a little sorry I didn't pick you up and carry you into the bedroom?"

His gaze reached into the center of her. How could she lie to those eyes? Why should she?

She swallowed past the lump in her throat, then whispered a throaty "Yes."

He sucked in a deep breath. "That'll get me through the rest of the night at least," he said huskily.

When he was gone, Ellie stood with her back against the door and stared at the opposite wall.

What was it about him, she wondered, that she found so hard to resist? She couldn't recall ever having responded so strongly to anyone else, ever having come so close to losing control.

The feeling frightened her. The kind of desire she felt for Mike bordered on love, and love itself was next door to the responsibility she'd avoided for so long.

She was no more ready for Mike Bannister and all that he represented than she was ready for the twenty-first century. But both seemed unstoppable. Time— and Mike—marched ever onward.

If she couldn't stop him and she wasn't ready for him, then what?

He who will, can.

Perhaps if she pledged to stand strong against him, she could.

At home, Mike blew his saxophone at the heavens, at the navy-blue sky, which was jammed with stars.

Tonight had been a mistake, all the way around. His euphoria from the Thompson win had driven him to Ellie, but he should have had better sense.

He'd known better. He'd felt from the beginning that he shouldn't rush her. Yet tonight he'd tried to. And he'd nearly ruined everything.

He couldn't afford to lose her. Not now when he was beginning to really care for her, beginning to let himself trust her.

Trust didn't come easy for him, especially not the kind of trust that would allow him to reveal himself the way he had tonight. Yet somehow Ellie had gotten past his reservations; somehow she'd worked around the doubts that had ridden him for so many years.

Perhaps because he was beginning to trust himself. Perhaps because he'd finally accepted that he alone controlled his destiny.

When he'd become a man, he'd left behind the suspicious child he'd once been. Perhaps now he was ready to be more: a man with a woman.

As he wrung "Basin Street Blues" from the sax, the memory of Ellie warmed him. He'd felt her desire tonight, felt her tremble from his caress.

He fully intended to take whatever steps were necessary to hold her again, to build that tremble to a full-blown quake. Soon. As soon as possible.

Under the heat of his breath, the saxophone cried its mournful notes into the night.

Six

An antique stained-glass lamp brightened the work area in front of Swan as Mike entered the reception area. He waited a second before she glanced up.

Then she frowned. "Mr. Bannister," she said. "Is Ellie expecting you?"

Somehow, when he'd made up his mind on the spur of the moment to talk with Ellie, Mike hadn't thought about what excuse he would use to see her. Now that he faced the problem, he felt a certain discomfort.

"Actually," he hedged, "I just stopped by to see how things were going." He wandered over to the desk and leaned against the edge. "So...how are they going?"

"As far as I know, *things* are great." She narrowed her slanted eyes. "Do you know something I don't?"

"Well..." A dozen ideas flitted through his mind, but he discarded most of them as he toyed with a glass paperweight from the desk. Inside was a small snow-covered Victorian house. He turned it upside down, then righted it and watched the snow drift down. Finally he said, "I think you two had a marvelous idea with this company."

Swan tapped the edge of a stack of papers against the desktop, aligning the edges. "We appreciate your compliments, and your recommendations. Buck Morgan's job may head us in a new direction."

After setting the paperweight back on the desk, he picked up a pewter letter opener lying next to the desk calendar. "It's a job that will work well for everyone. Buck was very impressed with your operation." Absently, he tapped the letter opener against the edge of the desk. "You've known Ellie a long time, haven't you?"

"Longer than anyone else in Dallas. Why?"

"Better, too, I guess." A slow, confident grin spread across his face. "But not as well as I'm going to," he said. He stabbed a square on the desk calendar that had been starred in red. "Was someone doodling, or is that date important?"

"Yes, ma'am," Ellie said into the telephone receiver. "I have all the information noted. Shall I read it to you again?"

"No, no," the elderly woman dithered. "I'm sure you'll handle everything quite well... as long as you remember what I said about the driver. My baby distrusts men, so the chauffeur must be a woman, and she should be quite plain, too, without makeup. Baby had a very bad experience with a groomer once...."

Ellie had already heard about several of the pampered dog's bad experiences. So, as her customer related this story one more time, Ellie knew exactly where to insert her murmurs of approval and tuts of regret.

Last night she had vowed to stand strong against Mike's charm; last night she'd believed she could. But already that strength had begun to weaken, and she hadn't even seen him.

Her mind was playing dirty tricks on her, taunting her with memories: the heat of his mouth, the excitement of his touch, the lure of his breath mingled with hers.

"Young lady? Young lady?"

The woman's sharp voice yanked Ellie out of her fantasies.

"Yes, ma'am," she said. "We'll see you tomorrow afternoon, 3:30 sharp."

As she hung up the phone, Ellie berated herself even harsher than her customer had. What in blazes did she think she was doing?

Fantasies be damned. Mike be damned. She had better things to do with her time than dream of Camelot. She had a business to run.

"You're a sweetheart," Mike told Swan. "I'll use the information well, I promise." He flipped his pen into the air, caught it with a snap, then tucked it back into his pocket.

He could see why Swan and Ellie were such good friends. They both had a gaiety that he envied, as if they knew a secret, shared some joke on the world that they weren't quite ready to reveal.

"Swan—" Ellie stood in the office doorway, her attention fixed on a piece of paper she held "—have you seen that list of—" She looked up at Mike and, for a minute, smiled. Then her smile disappeared.

Seeming uncomfortable under his scrutiny, she re-tucked a loose strand of hair into the coil at the back of her head, twitched her collar straight, then pulled off her glasses and chewed on the stem. "Did you want to see me?"

"If you've got a minute."

That hide-and-seek smile of hers was getting to him. What game was she playing now?

"I think I can find a minute." She gestured toward her office. "Come in." Inside she put her desk between them.

But Mike didn't take the chair across from her; he sat on the edge of her desk.

"You wanted something?" she asked.

"Yep."

"Well...?"

"We-ll," he drawled, dragging the word into two syllables, "how about lunch?"

"I've eaten."

"Then take a walk with me."

She arched a questioning eyebrow.

"Exercise is good for you," he said. "Besides, I'd like to talk with you, away from the office."

* * *

Ellie felt like a teenager playing hooky. Mike took her to Turtle Creek, one of her favorite spots in the city, where the sun spilled a golden puddle over the azaleas that flourished beside the winding creek, and the wind teased both of them with the scent of freshly mown grass and newly bloomed flowers.

"Someday," she told him as they walked beside the banks of azaleas, "mine will be this big, this lush."

"Only if you stop using it as a landing pad," he teased her.

She scowled at him. "It's not polite to remind a lady of her clumsiness."

"But you looked so cute in the brambles."

Sure she did, she thought, but she said nothing. For a while they strolled in silence.

Then Mike said, "I meant what I said last night. I really do like you." He plucked a leaf from a bush and twirled it in his fingers. "And I'd like to see more of you."

She winced. "I'm not sure that's a good idea. We're so different—"

"That's part of the charm," he said. "For me, anyway."

His choice of words jolted her. "That's exactly what I mean. Charm, luck, fate. You're preoccupied with fantasy," she complained as if she hadn't spun a few fantasies of her own. "And I'm a realist. As far as I'm concerned, luck is a four-letter word."

He laughed, as if she'd made a joke. Only she was as serious as sin.

"Luck's a fact of life; so's fate," he argued. "Just ask anyone who couldn't afford a seat on the *Hindenburg*."

"That wasn't luck; that was chance."

"Same thing. You could call my stumbling on to you chance, too, but I call it luck." He stopped beside her. "Whichever way, how about taking a chance on me?"

She wasn't arguing chance, only fate. She was no stranger to chance. When push came to shove, she would admit that coming to Dallas had been a risk, and so had starting the Genies. The safe thing would have been for her to stay in El Paso and work at the bank.

But Mike was a bigger gamble than she'd ever taken. Being near him was risky, scary and exciting all at the same time. There was so much to risk—so much to lose.

She wasn't concerned solely for herself. She feared for him as well. He trusted her, saw her as a lucky charm. And she knew how false that was.

Yet how could she walk away from him? Already he meant more to her than a client, more than merely a friend.

She sucked in a sigh and swallowed her fears. Would she take a chance on him?

Try to stop her.

A breeze off Lake Texoma riffled Ellie's hair, rustled the tree leaves and teased the bobbers in the lake, sending soft waves spiraling outward. In faded chinos and a bright yellow T-shirt, she sat cross-legged on the grassy shore, her fishing pole clasped loosely in her hands.

A few feet away, Mike leaned against a tree, his battered felt hat tugged down over his forehead. If Ellie hadn't known better, she'd have thought he was asleep.

But she knew better. The sleepy guise was a trick for the fish, a trick that six crappie had already fallen prey to.

Six! And she'd caught none. Not that she was competing with him, but she knew this spot, had fished it time and time again, and she'd always been lucky here.

She shook her foot, jiggling her pole. She might not believe in luck, but that had never kept the fish from biting before.

But perhaps if she played by Mike's rules... She closed her eyelids halfway and let her thoughts float formlessly.

The fish weren't her main purpose for fishing, anyway; she had hoped the beauty of nature would ease her mind, could help her forget the niggling problems of the Genies and the payroll and the weeds in her garden and the yellow leaf she'd found on her azalea.

Mike plucked a twig of grass, reached over and tickled her nose. "You know," he said lazily, "it's about time you learned to whistle."

She peered at him through one narrowed eye. She didn't want to learn to whistle, wasn't the least bit interested in it. Mainly because she knew she couldn't; she'd accepted that a long time ago, the same way she'd accepted certain other failings.

"First thing you do," he told her, "is pucker up. Come on, Ellie. Give it a try."

To humor him, she puckered. That much she could handle.

"Now—curl your tongue."

She truly tried. But her tongue felt like a resisting slab of meat.

"Now blow."

Although she made up in force what she lacked in technique, she still only managed to blow out a forceful raspberry.

Mike chuckled. "I don't think you've quite mastered the curl yet."

"Tongues don't curl."

"Yes they do. See?" He stuck out his tongue and curled it as if it were thin-sliced pastrami!

Exasperatedly she pursed her lips again and tried to duplicate his curl. Her tongue remained unwieldy, and nothing happened.

"I guess it's going to take some practice," Mike said. "But—" He pulled her toward him, meeting her in the middle. "I don't believe in wasting puckers," he said, then kissed her.

She forgot her pucker and her raspberry; she forgot her whistle and her pole, her bobber and her empty fish bucket. She forgot everything but Mike's kiss.

His lips conquered hers without a battle. She yielded willingly to his caress, ceding the warmth of her mouth to the probe of his tongue, to the electricity that started fires within her.

Then he drew away.

She knew it was for the best. But, when around him, acting for the best had become one of the hardest things she'd ever had to do.

After lunch, they sat in a tree-filled backyard that sloped down to the lake, and Mike told her lengthy, silly, charming stories about his childhood in the oil fields.

A bluebird perched on the edge of a birdbath; a butterfly flitted above the crocuses; an orange kitten ambled around the corner of the house.

When the cat spotted the bird, it began to slink. Frowning, Ellie picked up a stone. Maybe she could scare either the bird or the cat....

But, as birds do, this one seemed to sense its danger and flew into a redbud tree. The cat began to serenely bathe its paw.

Mike stretched out and gestured toward the cabin behind them. "Do Swan and Clement get to use their cabin much?"

"Not as much as they thought they would when they bought it."

"It's too bad they couldn't have come with us." He took the stone from her hand, tossed it up and caught it. Then, with a wink, he lobbed it into an oleander bush.

The leaves rattled. The kitten twitched its ear toward the sound.

Mike chucked another stone into the same oleander.

The cat looked over its shoulder, toward the bush.

Again Mike pitched a stone.

This time the cat turned its haughty stare on him.

"You have its attention, anyway," Ellie said.

"Give me a minute." He pulled his car keys from his pocket and dangled them close to the ground.

The kitten bathed its rear paw.

Ellie chuckled.

He dug into his pockets again. This time he pulled out a scrap of paper, wadded it and pitched it toward the cat.

The cat leaped at the wad, batting it. Then it bit into the paper, shook it, dropped it and slapped it again, chasing it across the yard.

"I'll bet it's a great mouser," Mike said approvingly.

When the chase brought the kitten near his chair, he picked it up, held it against his chest and petted it. It curled up in his lap. "Did you ever have a kitten?" Mike asked.

"I had a bird once," she said. "But birds and kittens don't mix." Neither had birds and Ellie, she thought.

"You're too irresponsible," Grandmamma had accused her. *"Pets require care. You can't even take care of a simple parakeet."*

The memory bit into her; tears threatened, and she swallowed them away. Her parakeet had been one of many things she couldn't take care of.

The cat jumped down, stretched forward and back, then sauntered away.

Mike stood.

"Where are you going?" Ellie asked.

"What if it doesn't have a home? Maybe it's a stray."

"Mike, there's probably a houseful of kids waiting for it right now."

He didn't sit down, but he did shove his hands into his pockets and wrinkle his brow thoughtfully.

"It looks well fed," she pointed out. "Wouldn't it be scraggly if it were a stray?"

Still scowling, he sat down. "In the oil fields," he said, "we collected strays. Stray dogs, stray cats, stray people." In answer to her questioning expression, he said, "Some of the best people I've ever known were considered strays by the rest of the world. Some of the best animals, too."

"Your childhood sounds...bohemian and unstructured. And marvelous. I envy you it."

His usually animated face stilled, and Ellie grimaced at her own tactlessness. She'd almost forgotten how unenviable he must consider his early life.

"I'm sorry, Mike. I wasn't thinking. I know it couldn't have been easy. You just make it sound that way."

"Fact of the matter is, it wasn't all that hard. Like a lot of people, most of the trouble I made for myself."

His attitude impressed her. Although many people were the cause of their own problems, few would accept the blame.

She did. She might never master whistling, but she was superb at accepting blame.

Clad in a pair of bright red shorts, a purple T-shirt and yellow sandals, Ellie turned another spadeful of soil. She'd bunched her hair on top of her head, first securing it with a large clip, then tying a rolled bandanna around her forehead, Willie Nelson style. Her official planting hat, a dilapidated straw, sat askew on her head.

She breathed in the sweet, loamy scent of the earth. Nothing, she thought whimsically, smelled better than dirt, except maybe rain.

But there was no promise of rain in the air today. Today Dallas had been blessed with sunshine. Not that she was complaining. It was beautiful weather for planting flowers, marvelous weather for celebrating a birthday, superstupendous weather for falling in love.

While she wasn't falling in love, today *was* her birthday, and these weren't weeds she was sweating over.

As far as love was concerned, though... She stabbed her spade into the earth.

In the past week she'd seen Mike practically every night and what had begun as a physical attraction had deepened into an abiding friendship. They'd searched out new restaurants to satisfy Mike's taste for exotic food, and he'd played his saxophone for her, wringing the blues from the horn until she almost cried with it.

They argued politics, too. He was a liberal—the kind that had abounded during the sixties. Although still a child at the time, he'd credited his mother with passing on the belief that the strong must take responsibility for the weak, the aged and the infirm.

Ellie didn't exactly disagree. But she believed in hard work. Her great-grandfather had struggled to build his banking empire, and his children had striven equally hard to keep it.

Their beliefs weren't incompatible, simply a bit dissonant.

With him, she felt caught between the devil and the deep blue sea. She still wasn't ready to accept love and the responsibility that came with it, but she cared too much to stop seeing him.

During the worst times as a teenager, when her guilt over her father had been almost overwhelming, when Grandmamma's sternness had seemed most accusing, determination had kept Ellie going. It would carry her through this as well; she'd see to that.

She wiped the back of her hand against an irritating itch on her cheek, then, her derriere resting on her heels, she potted the last bunch of petunias.

Mike hadn't been able to teach her to whistle, but if she allowed herself she could probably learn a great deal else from him. It was a big if.

Many people lived lifetimes without being tested, spans of years without having to face, much less live with, their inadequacies. How serene it must feel to remain blinded to reality. Ellie envied that serenity.

Pushing herself up, she carried her gardening paraphernalia to the backyard. First, she promised herself, she'd have a cool glass of lemonade, then a long, hot bath.

But once she was inside, the doorbell rang. She peeked out the front window and saw a florist van parked at the curb, then opened the door to a deliveryman with an armload of flowers.

He looked surprised for a moment as she stood there, and she fidgeted with her hair. It was probably a mess, but she didn't care.

"Yes?" she said.

"Ellie Logan?"

"Yes."

"These are for you." He handed her three wrapped bunches of violets and a box of yellow roses.

"Just a moment." As she searched for her purse, she wondered who might have sent the flowers. She'd told no one about her birthday; only Swan and their secretary knew.

When she returned with a tip, the man held two new bouquets.

"More?" she said incredulously.

His gaze locked again on her face for a fraction of a second before he looked away. "Lady, that ain't the half of it."

His remark didn't quite register as she dug into a bouquet of tulips for a card. She kicked the door closed.

He caught it with his foot. "Don't you want the rest of them?"

"The rest of what?"

He'd already started back to his van. When he returned, he carried another load of flowers. Then he went back for yet another. After the fourth trip, her entire living room was flooded with them: violets, daisies, daffodils, tulips, roses. The room looked like a greenhouse without the glass walls, with flowers stuck in vases, drinking glasses, mixing bowls and peanut-butter jars.

Finally he brought what he claimed to be the last bunch. "Where do you want these?"

"In there." She waved him toward a door in the hall.

He entered the room, stuck his head back out, and said, "Lady, this is—"

"Put them there, anyway."

"You're the boss." Again his glance seemed to fasten momentarily on her cheek before he slid it away.

When he was gone, she peered into the bathroom mirror, sucked in a sigh and let it out in a laughing groan. Her hair was horribly disheveled, but worse than that, there was a dirt streak down her cheek. She was still scrubbing it off when Mike walked in.

"Anybody home?"

"In here," she answered.

"Your front door was open." He stepped in the doorway, grinning, one hand hidden behind his back. Then, with a flourish, he produced a bunch of lilacs. "Have some flowers."

"*Some* flowers? Did you do this?"

Mike peered at the violet-filled sink and the toilet tank, into which roses and daffodils had been stuffed, and shook his head. "I don't think I would have been that inventive."

"Necessity's child," she admitted. "The living room overflowed."

"Really?" He wandered in there.

She followed.

"It looks ... springy," he said.

"Springy, my great-aunt Hilda. It looks crowded. Didn't anyone ever teach you moderation?"

"You think I overdid it?"

"I wasn't sure with the first load, or the second. I might not have even thought so with just a living-room full. But are there any left at the florist?"

"I was afraid I'd overdone it a little," he said seriously. "I seem to have trouble knowing when enough's enough."

But his mouth twitched with his apology. Obviously he was dying to laugh; obviously he would, given half the chance.

She didn't give it to him; she was too curious to indulge him yet. "How did you know today's my birthday?"

"Would you believe a bird told me?"

"A Swan, I suppose. Look, I do appreciate the flowers—"

"They're not just for your birthday, you know. You're the best good-luck charm I've ever had."

Disappointment rose in her, but it was her own fault. She should have left well enough alone—should have pretended the flowers were simply a birthday gift.

"What happened this time?" she asked with exaggerated patience.

"You remember that glass factory you told me about? The one that made your vase? Well, I bought some of the stock. And yesterday, it split! I hadn't invested enough to retire on, but it paid for your flowers several times over. Another bit of good luck."

If her birthday had been the only occasion, Mike might have sent a dozen flowers, not a roomful, and she would have been ecstatic.

"I never suggested that you invest in that company; I had no idea you were even going to. I'm not," she finished, her voice tinged with sarcasm, "a good-luck charm. When are you going to realize that?"

"When are you going to stop protesting and accept that for me you're lucky?"

"And when I'm not anymore? What then? Will it be my *fault* then?"

"I thought we'd settled that at the racetrack." He sat on the couch and pulled her down beside him. "You're overreacting. I'm not asking you to be responsible for me."

"Still…" She paused. "These past two weeks, that was all for CinderEllie, wasn't it? You were wining and dining your good-luck charm."

"You know that's not true. The good luck, that's just one part of the Ellie we all know and love. These past two weeks have been for the whole shooting match."

He stood and tweaked her hat lower onto her forehead. "So get out your fancy clothes tonight, love. I'm taking the shooting match out to celebrate."

Seven

By that night, Ellie shone, both in her clothing and her spirit. Challenging Mike's reason for sending the flowers, she decided, was mean spirited and very like checking a gift horse's teeth. If nothing else, he was an openhearted and appreciative man, and she should accept him as he was.

So, in a straight white silk chemise that was covered from neckline to hem with white crystal beads, she joined him for chateaubriand at Daniel's, a restaurant on McKinney Avenue.

He kept her laughing throughout dinner, making wry comments about their surroundings and the other guests.

And her retorts were as quick as always when with him—his remarks sparking hers, and hers his.

After one exchange, Ellie tried to bite back her laughter. After all, the atmosphere at Daniel's was elegant and sedate.

"I love the way you laugh—" Mike began, but was interrupted when a woman spoke his name.

He glanced up at an older woman standing a few feet away.

"Mother." He sounded both surprised and pleased.

The woman was tall and slender with curly, rust-colored hair. Beside her stood a man who was slightly taller than her.

Mike introduced his parents—Audrey Bannister and Ed Davis—to Ellie, then said, "I thought you were out of town, Dad."

"I got back last night." Ed Davis was lean and tough looking, his salt-and-pepper hair the only hint that he was old enough to be Mike's father.

"Why don't you two join us?" Mike suggested.

"Well—" Audrey glanced at Ed, then smiled "—okay, but we can only stay a moment. I'm really glad to meet you, Ellie," she said as they sat down. "I've heard so much about you."

After the waiter had brought coffee, she went on, "Mike says you own your own business. So do I."

While the two men discussed oil and the economy, Audrey described her interior-design company. She seemed to be listening to Mike and his father as well, because at the first break in their conversation, she said, "Your father's thinking about retiring, Mike."

Mike raised an eyebrow.

"I think I might," his father said, "if things keep going the way they already are."

"What about Davis Oil?"

Ed shifted in his chair, as if uncomfortable. "I'm considering splitting the stock between David and Sarah." Then his apparent discomfort vanished and he gave Mike a rock-jawed look. "You've always been a credit to me. Now I have to give David a chance to step out of my shadow." He paused. "I believe he can do it, given the chance."

"I think it's a good idea," Mike told him. "Especially the part about your retirement."

"We'll see. Right now it's just in the planning stages. Mainly it's going to depend on how well David and Sarah can accept your mother in my life. And don't think I don't know how spitefully they've treated you, too."

"It doesn't matter," Mike insisted.

But Ellie knew it did; even now she sensed the tension in Mike as his father forecast better times. Hidden by the drop of the tablecloth, she covered his fist with her hand and squeezed it.

"It would bother most people," Ed said. "They are your brother and sister."

"Half."

"Nevertheless," his father replied.

Mike and Ellie left shortly after his parents did. On the way home, neither commented on the moment in the restaurant when Mike had reacted to the mention of David's and Sarah's vindictiveness.

Once they were in her house, he tunneled his fingers through his hair—curly like his mother's, dark like his father's—and said, "How about a drink?"

He stood before the living-room window when she returned from the kitchen. The tiny creases on his forehead and around his mouth had deepened. Somehow, she knew, something about the encounter with his parents still bothered him.

She handed him his drink and sat on the sofa. "Would you like to talk?"

He joined her, sprawling into the opposite corner. "I think I would." He took a hefty swallow of Scotch. "I'm just not sure where to start." He regarded the drink in his hand, then began. "I'm not jealous, you know. At least I don't think so. I'd like for my mother to be able to get along with all of Dad's children. It would make things so much easier for her and Dad both."

There was an uncharacteristic awkwardness about him, almost a tentativeness. So Ellie allowed him to speak in his own time, his own way.

"It's old news now," he said, "but for a while in the sixties, Mother and I were headlined in every sleazy paper across the country. Everyone's sympathy was with Lucinda and her children. There was none left over for us."

She touched his knee but still said nothing.

"It was hard on both families, though I understand Lucinda at least knew all about us. She'd been ill for a long time and more or less allowed Dad his freedom, I've been told. But Sarah and David didn't know; finding out Dad had two families was as much of a shock for them as it was for me."

He seemed so far away from Ellie. It was as if he'd retreated to a long-ago time.

"I think you're extraordinary," she told him, "to try to understand how they feel. Not everyone would."

He shrugged. "I know how traumatic it must have been for them; it was bad for me, too. But my understanding's never made a difference before."

"Your parents seem to be working out their problems," Ellie pointed out.

"Lucinda's death allowed them that. I doubt Dad would ever have left her. He honored that part of his commitment; he continued to accept responsibility for her and supervised round-the-clock care for her."

Ellie knew only too well the heaviness of responsibility and the guilt one bore when it was mishandled.

Mike squeezed her hand, then let it go. He stood up and crossed over to her bookcase. "Your collection fascinates me." He picked up a millefiori paperweight, a clear glass globe that held suspended bouquets of brilliantly colored glass flowers, and he turned with it in his hands. "You can tell a great deal about people from their hobbies and collections." He carefully repositioned the paperweight. "Your paperweights speak of elegance but not distance. They're beautiful, yet they can be touched." He smiled with an offhandedness belied by the intensity in his eyes. "Can you be touched, Ellie?"

Her stomach flip-flopped, and her heart fluttered. She had been touched by Mike in so many ways. She followed him to the bookcase, then placed her palms on either side of his face.

"By you, I can," she whispered.

Sighing roughly, he pulled her into his arms. "I've wanted you so badly, for so long. There's not an inch of me that doesn't ache for you."

Determination seemed to have replaced his earlier uncertainty. Now he was sinew and bone in her embrace, rock and steel, a perfect foil to her softness.

Brushing her fingers through his hair, she lifted her face until her lips were a breath away from his. With a slow curl of her tongue, she traced the lower edge of his mouth.

She thrilled to the feel of him, thrilled at the sensations charging her body. Tendrils of heat, threads of desire, spiraled through her, tightening into a knot of longing. She'd never wanted anything as much in her life as she wanted him now, never felt so lacking yet so close to being filled.

"I've got to have you," he said, gripping her shoulder. "Let me love you, please?"

His plea reached deep within her, entwining her in fantasies of love that lived, love that was shared, love that was real. She knew such fantasies were naive, but for this moment Mike had helped her forget that. For just this moment she felt so close to him that she could almost believe any dream was possible. She led him down the hall and into her darkened bedroom.

His hands shook as he fumbled with the fastenings of her dress. He laughed self-mockingly. "I can't even make my fingers work." But when she tried to undo the buttons herself, he whispered, "No, let me."

Once the dress was finally unfastened, he slid it off her. The revolutions of the ceiling fan brushed fingers of air across her, and her body tautened with anticipation.

He left her on the bed for a moment. She heard the rasp of a zipper, the rustle of clothing, then the bed sank beneath him.

Clasping her head, he wove his fingers through her hair. "Can you feel me trembling, Ellie?" He brought her hand up to his chest. "Feel."

"I can feel your heartbeat." She moved her fingers over the muscles of his chest, her breath catching in her throat. "But you're not the only one trembling."

With his tongue, he explored her ear, then the tendons down the side of her throat. Finally he reached her breast and, with a slow, sensuous swirl, he sipped at her nipple. She whimpered.

He kissed her as if he could never get enough, as if he could never be satisfied.

She couldn't. She knew she couldn't, but still she clung to him as if perhaps she could if she held on tightly enough.

When she thrust her tongue into his mouth, he captured it, toyed with it. He slid a hand down her back and pressed her to him, so that she felt the full strength of his desire.

"You feel so good," he breathed.

His mouth was so close, so tempting. Again she tasted him, again slipping her tongue into the depths of his mouth, in and out, in a reproduction of an act more intimate, more intense. Finally she could stand the agony no longer.

"Please, Mike," she murmured.

He pushed himself between her legs, his thigh pressing against the softness of her. He groaned.

"I've been almost afraid to touch you," he said. "Afraid you'd disappear." He brushed his mouth over her cheeks, her chin, and down the curve of her neck. "You won't, will you?"

Raking her nails along his back, down to the base of his spine, and beyond, she whispered, "Trust me."

He arched into her.

She gasped. And gasped again. Never had she been so complete, so full. Her sensations took her past the edge of reason. All that mattered was Mike. Nothing else was important.

With each stroke, she burned hotter. Every thrust took her higher, and she murmured senseless, meaningless sounds of love to him.

He took her farther and farther. To the future and beyond. When she reached the edge of forever, her body burst into shudders, shivering with a convulsive energy that she'd never known before. She curved into him, bowing upward, tightening every muscle in her body with her release.

He moaned harshly above her, and she dug her fingertips into him, sharing his moment vicariously. Then he wrapped her tightly around him as they slid, gently, slowly, back to this moment.

Afterward, in the sweet fullness of satisfaction, he curled himself around her. "Ellie, sweet, sweet Ellie." He toyed with a strand of her hair, then nudged her cheek with his nose and nibbled on her chin. "I can't believe you're so beautiful." He stroked his hand down her thigh. "So soft."

"Don't we fit nicely?"

"Superstupendously." He cupped a derriere cheek in each of his hands, almost hefting them.

She laughed and twisted away from him, ending up in the middle of the bed in a half-lotus position.

He pushed two pillows behind his back and sat up, folding an arm behind his head. "Talk to me," he said. "Tell me something about yourself."

"Like what?"

"Like—what were you like as a child? You never talk much about your childhood."

"Don't I?" She propped her elbows on her knees. "I guess I don't, do I? What do you want to know?"

He tweaked a strand of her hair. "Did you wear pigtails?"

"Until I was around eleven or twelve. Then I decided I was too old. You see, after my mother died, I sort of took over as the lady of the house."

"Kind of young, isn't it?"

"I didn't think so. I took over the whole operation, gave orders to the housekeeper and the gardener both. And they went on, doing just what they did before Mamma died. But they let me think it was my superior management that carried us through the rough times."

She had believed she was responsible for all the times things turned out well, so she'd never allowed herself to shrug off the blame for the times they hadn't. Especially that last time.

Perhaps then, if she'd been wiser or older or anything but plain, ordinary Ellie Logan, perhaps then things would have turned out differently. Possibly her father would still be alive. If only...

But regret couldn't bring Daddy back, though she knew she'd never forget the tragedy of his death. Nor would she ever allow herself to carry that kind of responsibility again.

Mike put his hand on her knee. "Sounds like your childhood wasn't a whole lot better than mine."

"How old were you when you found out about your father?"

"Nine. It's not an easy age for a boy, anyway, and the publicity didn't help. And there were plenty of snooty better-than-thou people in the small town where I grew up." He leaned on his elbow. "Sometimes when they looked so coldly down their noses at me I'd pretend icicles were dripping from their nostrils. Then they stopped being scary and became funny."

Ellie hurt for him. She pictured him in childhood, so vulnerable to adult opinion, slapped down by vicious gossip and sensational headlines. She wished she could go back and fix it for him, go back and punch a few icy noses.

"If only I had your kind of imagination," she said. "I've faced more upturned noses than you might think, and sticking icicles on them would've helped immensely."

"Nobody would snub you."

"Don't you believe it. We all have our ghosts. Me included."

"What's yours?"

She wasn't ready to tell him. Not the whole of it. Although he had confided in her, somehow she wasn't ready to do the same; her wounds hadn't yet healed. Perhaps they never would.

"I was an ugly duckling?" she ventured.

"Can't be that. Must've been something else." He reached up and traced the swell of her breast. His touch ignited a new fire in her.

When he tugged on her hand and pulled her down into his arms, she wrapped her thighs around his leg and held on tightly. She wanted him again so badly her nipples beaded from the mere thought of it.

He crushed her mouth with his kiss and traced her body with the heat of his hands, branding her with his touch.

She burned for him. In their joining before she'd felt so complete; she wanted that feeling back.

"I need you," she whispered. "Now."

He entered her quickly, and she arched into him, compelled by desire, by need, by emotion. He drove fiercely into her.

She returned his ferocity, emboldened by the frenzy of their combined passion. She dug her fingernails into his back, as if by force she could pull every particle, every ounce, of love from him.

He pushed deeper and deeper into her, but Ellie demanded more; she wanted all of him, wanted to *be* Mike and for him to be her.

At the very moment she reached her pinnacle, he exploded inside her.

Then, sated, she lay in his arms. Under the spell of his touch, all the heartbreak, all the loneliness that had been a part of her for so long disappeared.

Nothing could hurt her while he was beside her. Nothing.

Eight

Stretched out in front of Ellie's fireplace, her elbow bent and her head supported by her hand, Swan slapped the cards onto the carpet. "Gin," she said smugly.

Ellie sat cross-legged on the floor with her back against a chair. "Wait a minute," she said, and she fanned Swan's cards. "You...cabbage leaf! If you had any sleeves, I'd be checking them."

"You think I'm cheating?"

"That's the problem." Ellie gathered the cards together and tossed the deck to her friend. "I know you're not. Okay, deal again."

Swan dealt the cards like a Las Vegas shark. "When's Mike supposed to be back?"

"On Saturday."

He had left for Arizona yesterday morning, and Ellie had had a devil of a time getting past her loneliness last night. So, when she learned that Swan's husband was at a sales conference in California, she'd convinced her friend to keep her company.

"I figured you'd be able to tell me when his plane would get here in minutes, seconds, all the way down to nanoseconds," Swan kidded her.

"Down to what?"

"Nanoseconds. It's a computer term. Means one billionth of a second."

Ellie wrinkled her nose. "You know what I think of computers. But that's not a bad word. Nanohungry... would that mean I was one billion *times* hungry or one billionth part of hungry?" Still considering the question but not expecting an answer, she held her cards up and spread them out, one at a time. "I could almost make it that exact, you know. When Mike'll be back, I mean. But I wouldn't want you to think I'm too eager."

Swan's face reflected a strained patience as Ellie took her time over the cards. "Even when I had to call you three times to get your attention yesterday, and you 'shushed' me and said you were Arizona dreaming, I didn't think you were too eager." Tapping her cards against her knee, she added, "I thought you were strange!"

When Ellie discarded a jack of clubs, Swan yelped, grabbed the card and stuck it into her hand, then threw down all her cards. "Knock!" she cried exultantly.

"That's it!" Disgusted, Ellie tossed her cards on top of Swan's. "I don't want to be a bad loser, but with you gin's not a nice, friendly game at all. With you, it's always attack and overthrow."

"Whatever works." Grinning, Swan unfolded her length from the floor. "I'm going to make another margarita. Want one?" She disappeared into the kitchen.

Ellie scooped up the cards, patted them together and stuck them into the drawer of a lamp table. "How long did it take you to get used to Clement being gone so much?" she called as she curled up on a tapestry-covered tub chair.

"I'll let you know if I ever get used to it," Swan said, returning with the drinks. "Even during the summer, the bed seems cold when he's gone. This time when he gets back, *we're* going somewhere, anywhere, as long as it's out of telephone reach of the Genies—no offense meant."

"As I recall, every year Clement fights you over your vacation."

"And every year I win. Want to know how?" Swan smiled as if she had a deck of cards up her non-existent sleeves. "All I have to do is get that man in bed, and he'll give me anything I want."

Ellie whooped a laugh. "Swan!"

"I *mean*, I get him in bed, and I snuggle up, and— you know that bald spot on top of his head—well, I rub that spot, and I say—" she lowered her voice until it was silky "—I say, 'Honey, baby, we *need* some time together.' And I rub, and I rub." She shrugged. "Works every time. You ought to try it."

"Mike doesn't have a bald spot."

"Rubbing works all over."

"I'm not trying to drag him off on vacation, either."

"It's good for practically anything. And bald spots aren't necessary. It's being close and being sweet and being—" she curled her mouth naughtily, wrinkling her nose "—impossible to say no to. Didn't your mother ever teach you anything like that?"

"I was too young when Mamma died, and fathers don't teach their daughters those kinds of things; at least mine didn't. And after he died...well, you know about after that. I doubt Aunt Julia ever got close to anyone's bald spot. Grandmamma would've fainted if anyone had ever suggested she rub *anything* of Grandpapa's."

"And then there's Aunt Edith."

Ellie chuckled. "If it hadn't been for her and her flamboyant personality, I might've become another Aunt Julia."

Swan shuddered. "Still, although I adore your Aunt Edith, she never did get married. You're not using her as a role model, are you?"

"I'm not, but I could choose worse."

"Are you afraid of marriage?"

Ellie rested her elbow on the arm of the chair, cupped her chin in her hand and considered the question. "I have a great deal of respect for the institution," she allowed, "but I'm not sure I want to be institutionalized."

Swan groaned.

"It may be an old joke, but it's appropriate."

Swan stuck her stockinged feet onto the coffee table. "Weren't your parents happy together?"

"I suppose so—I mean I guess they were." Ellie paused. Then she asked, "How much does a kid really know?"

"Usually more than adults give them credit for, I think. Like my Aunt Jessica. She'd have her 'iced tea' every morning without fail and rave about how it must be made so properly," Swan said. Then she snorted. "Aunt Jess's hundred-proof 'tea' killed her when I was ten, and even then my grandmother swore Jess's womb had done the dirty deed."

A typical Southern cover-up, Ellie thought. "As far as my parents go," she said, "I don't really know if they were happy together, but I do remember my dad was lost without my mother."

"Well, my dad *prayed* to be lost every now and then," said Swan.

"If your mother's as sneaky as you, I can understand that."

"I'm not sneaky! I'm resourceful." Swan held up her drink. "Watch how the light changes the green. Makes it even mintier looking. Sure doesn't *taste* minty, though." She sipped the margarita, as if she were testing to make sure. "You've never said much about that period right after your mother died. Did you try to take over for her?"

"No one could have," Ellie told her. "Mamma was one of a kind. I mean, she knew how to handle my father. He'd get some of the wildest ideas, and she seemed to know exactly which ones to let him run with and which ones to weed out."

Ellie stared into her glass. She wasn't studying the color, didn't really care at the moment if her drink was purple. Instead she was remembering the old feelings of inadequacy. She could never have lived up to her mother, not if her father had lasted a hundred years longer, rather than only two. "Mamma's thumb *glowed* green when it came to Daddy's ideas," she said.

"And yours didn't."

Her laugh was dry, self-mocking. "Are you kidding? I can tend an azalea better than I could Daddy. When it came to him, my thumb was browner than your skin." She paused. "Did I ever tell you that you have pretty skin?"

"Yep," Swan said. "I think it was last time we talked about your childhood. Couldn't be an evasion, could it?"

"You *do* have pretty skin. You're a beautiful woman, Swan Stephens."

"And you're a tough one, Ellie. Want another drink?"

"Maybe we'd better switch to coffee. Unless you want to spend the night."

"I'd only be trading my cold bed for your cold couch. We'd better make it coffee."

The next evening, Ellie's dinner for one was indescribably lonely. The telephone call Mike had made to her the night he left was now no more than a faint memory.

What had she done with her evenings before he'd come along?

She had a whole slew of friends she could call; one would surely go to dinner with her. But dinner alone sounded better right now than being sociable.

So she stayed home, with the nostalgia station on cable. Dinner was a glass of milk, a few wheat crackers and some Swiss cheese, shared with Charles Boyer and Jennifer Jones.

Somewhere between the end of *Cluny Brown* and the start of the next feature, she decided to make popcorn. It had reached the briskly popping stage when the phone rang. Still shaking the pan, she scrambled for the receiver. "Yes," she said.

"Ellie?"

"Mike! Just a minute." She laid the receiver on the counter, then carried the pot of still-popping corn over to the sink.

When she returned to the phone, her voice had dropped several decibels. "Mike," she said breathily, "I'm so glad you called."

"I told you I would when we talked Monday night, didn't I?"

She didn't remember him saying so, and she was sure she would have. But it didn't matter. "I'm still glad you did."

"Have you missed me?"

Like a drowning man misses air, she thought. But, not ready to tell him that, she said, "Who, me? I'm having a grand time."

"Try not to have *too* grand a time. Because I'm missing you. Can't you miss me a little?"

"Maybe I'll give you a teeny tiny nanomiss."

"A teeny tiny what?"

She laughed. "Never mind. So you're missing me? I like the sound of that."

"It's been rough here without you," he said. "I could sure use your magic. If something could go wrong, it has."

Disappointment rushed through her. More than disappointment; she felt almost abandoned. She'd let herself believe that she was more to him than a good-luck charm. Fool that she was.

"I'm sorry things aren't going well for you," she said, her voice tight, "and I really hate to cut this off, but you caught me at an inconvenient time."

"Were you taking a bath?" His voice was low, husky, twenty-four-karat sexy, and the sound of it liquefied her lower body.

But not her head. Her brain was out of melting range, barely out, but still, right now, it was the center of her pain. "I was just...busy."

"Ellie? Did I say something wrong?"

What good would it do to tell him how she felt? They'd been over this luck issue so many times before, obviously to no avail.

"Really, Mike, I do need to go. I'll see you when you get back." Without waiting for a response, she hung up.

He called her the next evening, and the evening after that. She deftly kept their conversations bright, brisk and friendly, avoiding any intimacy. By Saturday she felt she'd built up enough resistance to manage their relationship exactly the same way. She'd value his friendship, as distantly as possible, and take pleasure in their amicable conversations.

Saturday afternoon she was outside washing windows when he pulled up at her curb. She waved and smiled nicely, politely, amicably.

He stepped out of the car, then reached back in and tugged out a puff of blue-gray fur.

"I brought you a present," he said when he reached her. He held out a purring kitten. "Her name is Fido." He grinned. "She thinks she's a dog."

Ellie shrank from the cat. "I don't care if she's a water buffalo. Send her back where she belongs."

"But she's a gift, for you."

Good manners had been an important part of Ellie's upbringing. She knew how to graciously accept a gift; she also knew her own limitations. This living creature needed a reliable, trustworthy owner. Ellie had no desire to take on that responsibility.

"I don't know the first thing about cats," she told Mike. "It isn't fair to Fido for you to leave her with me."

"You don't like kittens?"

"I wouldn't know what to do with her."

"Ellie," Mike said, emphasizing the last syllable soulfully. His eyes were soulful, too, but Fido's weren't. *She* gazed at Ellie steadily, haughtily, as if she knew she held the upper hand.

"You don't have to do anything special," he assured her. "Just feed her, love her, clean out the litter when she messes up."

"See! I don't know how to clean out litter. And what am I supposed to feed her? Milk? Caviar?"

"No, not—"

"And what if she gets sick? What do I do then? What about distemper? Leukemia? What if she gets pregnant?"

"That's what veterinarians are for. Here, you carry Fido inside while I get her things out of the car." He slid the cat into her arms.

She sucked in a disbelieving sigh as Fido eyed her disdainfully. Mike might think veterinarians were the answer, but Ellie was certain that if she kept this cat, she'd do the fretting. Her parakeet had been lost because of her, and she hadn't been able to keep her father from dying. How in blazes could she take care of a helpless cat?

"Just give it a try," Mike called over his shoulder. "A few days, that's all."

"Come on, Ms. Hoity-toity," Ellie said through gritted teeth, "into the house with you." She carried the lump of fur into the living room and then let go, emphatically.

Fido landed on her feet and backed away, with her head lowered and her back arched in classic cat fashion.

"I'm not all that fond of you, either," said Ellie, holding her ground.

"Where shall we set this up?" Mike stood in the living-room doorway. "The utility room?"

She wrinkled her nose at the litter box. "Let's talk about this."

"Okay, but I know for a fact she hasn't been near anything resembling a litter box since early this morning. And I'd hate for anything to happen to that cream-colored carpet of yours."

She sank onto the couch. "All right. Put it wherever you think best."

Mike left, and Fido followed, her tail waving like a banner. Ellie stayed behind. She wouldn't have another moment of peace until she could convince Mike to repossess the cat, tie a ribbon around its neck and give it to his mother—or someone.

"Anyone," she muttered.

"What did you say?" He walked back in, Fido on his heels.

"I said, I think she likes you." Ellie smiled sweetly. "Doesn't she?"

"Yes, and I couldn't leave her. She's acted like this since the first time I saw her. Like a dog, the way she followed me around all week."

"You brought her from Arizona?"

Mike sat down. Fido sprang onto his lap, curled into a ball and purred...loud enough for all of Dallas County to hear.

"Didn't I say that?"

Ellie hadn't thought Fido could purr any louder, but she was wrong. When Mike rubbed the cat between the ears her purr revved up, sounding like a horde of Hell's Angels.

"She's not very old, barely past weaned," Mike said. "And when she jumped in the back of the pickup truck this morning, I couldn't leave her behind.

"I understand that, I really do. But you should keep her, Mike, not me. She's crazy about you. And I don't know beans about cats."

Mike's gaze caught hers and, as always, her foundations crumbled. He hadn't been able to refuse Fido and she—blast and be damned—couldn't refuse him.

"I wanted you to have her because I missed you, and because you missed me, too, whether you'll admit it or not...."

His tone of voice had about the same effect that his eyes had: her stomach floundered; her heart tap-danced. He could play her like his saxophone and make her feel as blue as it sounded.

"...And because you seemed to be angry with me...."

"I wasn't," she began. Then she stopped. She was certain he knew she had been, even if she wasn't now.

"...And because I love you," he finished softly.

This time her belly turned over and her mouth dropped open, as if she were some backwoods country girl at a French fashion show.

He was in love with her? Hope rose inside her, and she tried to squelch it. She wanted so badly to believe him, but fear held her back. She wouldn't always spell luck for him, and what happened when that was gone?

"Aren't you going to say anything?" he asked.

"Did you have good weather flying back? How'd you get Madame here onto the plane?"

"Alan Thompson flew me back in his plane. Did you hear what I said?"

"I'm not mad at you, you know."

"Ellie?"

She fiddled with a strand of her hair as she studied his face. "I think you need me," she murmured.

"Needing's part of loving."

"I mean, I think you have the idea that I'm your lucky charm."

He stood, dumping Fido from his lap. The cat landed on her feet, lucky cat. Ellie knew she didn't have a chance in a hundred of faring as well if Mike ever dumped her. Somehow, though, the possibility merely mocked her; she wouldn't allow it to scare her away.

He pulled her up off the couch and into his arms. "I'm in love with plain, ordinary Ellie Logan. She's the one I need to be with—" he grinned "—plain, ordinary me."

Heaven help her, she believed him. "I'll give you plain, ordinary," she breathed just before he kissed her.

"Ahh, Ellie," he groaned against her mouth. "Being away from you was pure hell. I don't even want to think about the next trip."

Still kissing her, he caught her face between his palms, holding her still as he plunged his tongue between her teeth. His hunger—and hers as well—was desperate, greedy, seeking.

"Now, Ellie," he declared, swinging her up into his arms. "I can't wait a moment longer." With long, confident strides, he carried her down the hall.

In the bedroom, they removed each other's clothing with eager, fumbling fingers, then fell into bed. He used his mouth and his tongue to caress her, adoring her shoulders and the soft curve of her inner arm as it led to her breast. He laved the swell of her breast until he reached the tip, then he circled her nipple with a heat-building swirl of wetness.

With a soft sigh, she took him in her hands, thrilling at the fullness, the strength of him. She wanted to give everything back to him, all the wetness, all the heat, all the love. She tightened her hand around him and drew her mouth downward.

He trailed his hand up her thigh, reached the heat of her and slipped a finger inside. She gasped weakly. His rhythm, his sliding, pulsing motion, took her breath away, stole her senses.

She moved with him, moaning, murmuring his name, whispering her love to him. He stroked her slowly, gently, until she thought she would die with the feel of it.

He filled her with his heat, his swelling, his love. She thrust her body upward, moving toward him, with him, gliding higher and higher.

Together they soared; together they flew until her world burst in a shower of laughing gray eyes, sparkling gray eyes, loving gray eyes.

In the peace that came afterward, she played with the hair on his chest. "I'm not mad, you know."

He laughed. "I think we've established that. But you were. Want to tell me why?"

"I thought you wanted me in Arizona because I'm lucky for you and things weren't going well."

"You are lucky for me, and things weren't going well." He tugged her closer. "But I wasn't asking you to change them; it just makes it easier for me when you're with me."

She grinned. "You had Fido."

"And now you have her."

"Mike, let's talk about that. I've never had a pet—"

"I thought you had a bird."

"I did once, but it flew away."

He shrugged, then with a teasing grin, said, "Oh, well, everyone knows birds are flighty." When she groaned, he went on, "Seriously, it's time you had a real pet."

"But...I don't know how."

"It's easy. You take life a day at a time, take care of the basics. That's all there is to it. Tend to Fido like you tend to your business."

"My business is an *impersonal* responsibility. Owning a cat's a very personal thing."

"Don't think of her as belonging to you. Think of her as a friend, as company when I'm not with you."

Ellie buried her face in his shoulder and muttered, "She'll depend on me. Entirely on me."

"Actually, cats are quite independent, and I'll help you with her. I promise. And if it doesn't work, I'll...I'll take her to my mother."

"Why couldn't you take her home with you? Now."

"I have to leave town too often. I'd hate to have to keep putting her in a kennel."

Ellie sighed. "All right. I'll try. But that's the best I can promise."

"That'll do for now." He nuzzled her neck. "If things go the way I hope," he said as he stroked the inside of her thigh slowly, teasingly, "maybe soon she'll be with me, anyway."

Ellie didn't like the sound of his implication. "What do you mean?"

"I love you; you love me, right? Right. So with one step following another... Don't you think it could?"

She didn't think, refused to think. She cared for Mike more than she'd ever allowed herself to care for anyone. But she hated for people to rely on her, and she liked her life the way it was. She quailed at the thought of taking on any personal responsibility.

Marriage, even living with someone, required a commitment she wasn't ready to consider.

Nine

It was a perfect day for a wedding.

June had exploded with a burst of color in the garden behind the house in University Park, and the soft green of the lawn formed a gentle background for the ceremony.

A breeze ruffled the leaves, and dappled patterns of sunlight filtered through, shifting like flowing water on the grass. A robin hopped across the lawn behind the altar, seemingly oblivious of the crowd watching the man and woman who stood before the minister.

Mike fidgeted. If he'd had his way, only the immediate family would be here. But it was a day he didn't want to spoil, so when the plans were being made, he had held his tongue and said nothing.

But with all the guests, what should have been a dignified rite had become a three-ring circus. He could tolerate worse than this, though, as long as he had Ellie by his side.

Throughout the exchange of the vows, he clung to her hand. His knees felt weak, his legs like Silly Putty.

When the minister said, "You may now kiss the bride," Mike's breath whooshed out almost audibly, as if he'd forgotten to breathe until now. They were married. Finally.

"Michael, darling."

Laura Morgan floated toward Mike and Ellie, the draped hem of her silk chiffon dress fluttering in the wind. Buck followed her.

"Your mother makes such a lovely bride," Laura gushed. "I'm almost tempted to do it again myself."

"You do, hon," Buck promised, "and you'll do it alone. I've said my vows before a preacher. Don't intend to do it again." He smiled at Ellie. "You met my wife, didn't you, Ellie? Laura, Ellie Logan."

Laura nodded and swept a dismissive glance over Ellie. "I haven't seen your brother and sister," she told Mike.

"You remember Ellie, don't you, Laura?" Buck insisted. "We met her at Nora Chapman's party."

"Of course." Again Laura nodded. "It's good to see you again." Then to Mike she said, "David and Sarah are going to be here, aren't they?"

The sweetly innocent expression that appeared on Ellie's face concerned Mike. In her cream silk dress she resembled an angel, but he didn't trust that look.

Before he could head her off, she said, "I served you champagne at that party. As a matter of fact, I served it all over you."

He stifled a groan. Now she'd done it. If Laura had anything to do with it, Ellie could kiss goodbye any new business she might have gotten from Buck.

"You—?"

Buck didn't seem upset. He broke in, laughing. "Of course that was Ellie. How could you forget?"

"Some things," Mike said quickly, "are best forgotten. Including that party." If threatening to expose Laura's seduction attempt would quell her vindictiveness, he'd use it in an instant. But he doubted it would. For now he simply wanted to get Ellie out of firing range. "I think Mother's trying to get our attention, Ellie. She probably wants me for the family pictures." He steered Ellie away. "I'm sure we'll see you both later."

After the wedding pictures had been taken, one of the guests spirited Mike away. Ellie stood alone now, under a ginkgo tree. She knew few of the guests, so she simply watched the festivities.

The men wore dinner jackets; the women were dressed in a variety of styles, from starkly tailored to softly sculptured. The colors splashed across the grass like a spring garden.

Almost a month had passed since her birthday, and with it had gone all her defenses. Gradually she'd begun to believe that possibly, if she tried hard enough, she might be able to handle personal responsibility without making a disaster of it. She wanted to believe it—needed to believe it. She could no more leave Mike than she could whistle.

Then, as if it were actually true, the thought of being without him stabbed through her.

She closed her eyes against the pain, and when she opened them, his mother had joined her. "Are you feeling all right?" she asked.

"I was just taking a breather," Ellie said. Then she complimented Audrey on the wedding, the garden and the sunshine. "And you look beautiful," she concluded.

"All brides seem to have a sheen about them, don't they? I can't decide whether that's love or perspiration." The older woman regarded Ellie thoughtfully. "Mike explained about us, didn't he?"

Ellie nodded. "Mike's proud of you both. And your being together makes him happy."

"I wish I could say as much for Ed's other children. But nobody ever said it would be easy." Audrey tapped her open hand against her skirt, then smiled. "Mike tells me you have a new cat."

"*He* has a cat. I'm keeping her for a while."

Audrey chuckled. "Famous last words. Take it from one who knows from experience—the cat is yours. How old is she?"

"About two months, and she is Mike's."

"But you're the one who feeds her in the morning, right? And at night." Audrey's hazel eyes danced. "Cats," she said, "like some men, have a direct connection between their stomachs and their hearts. Believe me. She's yours."

"She deserts me the minute Mike walks in the door."

"And comes back the minute he walks out; I know, it's happened to me. Who does she sleep with?"

"She has no choice; it's me or no one."

Except, Ellie corrected herself silently, on the nights Mike stays over. She wasn't sure who liked those nights better—she or Fido.

"I think you're hooked, and I'm an old hand at it. Like it or not, that cat's— Oh, my stars," Audrey breathed. "Look who's here." She nodded toward where Mike and his father stood near a small camellia-filled pond near the house.

With them was a man, short and fortyish, with thick, almost cotton-white hair and a mustache. He was accompanied by a sleek, golden-haired woman.

Audrey nudged Ellie forward. "I think we're needed. Right now."

"Who are they?" Ellie asked, following. "What's going on?"

"Just a minute and I'll introduce you." When they came into hearing range of the others, Audrey said, "David, Sarah, how sweet of you to come. Isn't it, Ed?" Taking her husband's arm, she introduced Ellie to Mike's half brother and sister.

"Ed was disappointed when he thought you weren't going to be able to be here. We're pleased you could make it."

"I take it everything's over," Sarah said matter-of-factly.

"You mean the ceremony?" Audrey's smile looked almost genuine. "It's a shame you missed it, but it was videotaped. We'll be happy to invite you over to see it when we return from Monaco."

"Homemade videos are so boring." Sarah curled her upper lip distastefully. As far as Ellie was concerned, the look the woman slid down her nose could have frozen Old Faithful. But Ellie didn't find the image of Sarah dripping icicles humorous; she fairly bristled from the woman's rudeness. "And Monaco... Daddy, really, why would you take her there? After all, Mother loved—"

"Sarah." David's voice held a warning, but otherwise everyone carefully ignored Sarah's rudeness.

"Monaco sounds wonderful." David, at least, seemed to be trying, Ellie mused. "When were we there last? I was about seventeen, wasn't I?"

"And Sarah was twelve." Ed hugged one arm around his daughter. "I hear you've spent some time there recently, so Audrey and I thought we'd give it a try. Now... why don't you go mingle?"

Sarah smiled tightly, as if she were afraid her face might crack. "Of course, Father. I saw the Morgans as I walked in. And there are some other... people here, aren't there? People I know."

"Get to know the rest," her father suggested. "Pretend you're running for governor."

"The yard looks beautiful," David said after his sister had left. "A perfect setting for a wedding. I hate that we missed it. But Sarah's never been known for her punctuality."

"My sister was like that," said Audrey. "Everyone teased her about it, but I found it one of her most charming traits. It was so... *un*stuffy."

"That's a positive way of looking at a character flaw," David said. "I've only just learned to tolerate it." He pulled thoughtfully at his mustache. "If you two want to visit with some of the other guests," he said, "I'd like to chat with Mike." He plucked a glass of champagne from the tray of a passing waiter. "We haven't talked in quite some time."

Ed's grin was approving. "It's about time you two got on friendly terms," he said. "And Audrey and I will introduce Ellie around."

Ellie knew her protective feelings for Mike were probably misplaced. Undoubtedly he could handle a tête-à-tête with his brother without her help, but she left reluctantly, glancing over her shoulder.

Mike had always felt an empathy for his siblings, even during the time when he'd been the one most affected by the publicity. He could almost have made their anger his. Their mother had been betrayed, while, in his child's eyes, his mother and he had been rejected. He knew David's and Sarah's anger and their hurt, too; he'd lived both.

"This is a big day for you, isn't it?" David said.

"I hope in time you'll be as pleased as I am. Obviously nothing can be changed."

"Obviously." David lifted his glass to his mouth. A ray of sunlight struck the crystal and burned hotly for a moment, glaring into Mike's eyes.

He looked away. "I'm glad to see you trying, at any rate. I'm sure it must be hard."

"There's no reason not to. Father stayed with Mother as long as she was alive. I might not have approved of his actions all those years, but I can't fault him for not leaving." David paused, then said, "I hear good things about your company, Mike. Congratulations."

Mike answered David's questions about Bannister Drilling openly, even talked about the Dunes well. As a gamble, it had paid off beautifully, and he was proud of it.

Neither of them mentioned Sarah, and for Mike the strain became awkward. He was beginning to believe that eventually David might accept him and his mother.

But Sarah was another matter altogether.

"I've always liked this house," David said. "My aunt...*our* aunt," he corrected, "used to live here, you know. You would have liked her, I think. She was very like Dad."

Finally Mike reached his tolerance level. "About Sarah..."

David shook his head. "I was hoping she'd at least be courteous," he said. "But maybe we're asking too much. Perhaps she needs more time to adjust. Sarah always takes longer to accept changes, but once she does, she accepts them wholeheartedly. When she was eight, her best friend moved away. Sarah sulked for two months, refused to even talk to the little girl who moved next door. She's still friends with the second one, and I doubt she even remembers the name of the first.

"She does listen to me, though," he went on. "More, at least, than she does to anyone else. And I'd like to see her accept Audrey. There's been too much division in this family for far too long."

On Sunday night, Ellie sat in the curl of Mike's arm, with Fido in his lap as they watched a late movie.

"What do you think your mother and father are doing right now?"

"Right now?" He checked his watch. "They're probably either sound asleep or in one of the casinos."

"I don't think they're doing either one," she said. "I think they're dancing under the Mediterranean stars—"

"Same stars we have here."

"Under *Mediterranean* stars, thick and blazing like diamonds. They're dancing all by themselves, and in the background an orchestra's playing Rachmaninoff." Her voice was low and dreamy. "The air smells like the sea and flowers, and your mother's wearing a long gown that flares out every time your father twirls her. And he's smiling down at her. Way down."

"Not too far down," Mike laughed. "He's not much taller than she is."

Ellie glared at him. She'd had a nice fantasy building, and he kept interjecting reality.

"Kind of like we are," he said, smiling—sort of—down at her.

"So much for fantasies."

"If I remember correctly, you told me you were a realist." He hugged her. "I hope I had something to do with the change. Keep dreaming, darling, but remember I love the pragmatic Ellie, too."

A few moments passed, then he said, "You know what I'd like to do?"

"Run away to the circus?"

"Run away, but not to the circus. Do you think you could take a week off?"

"That depends. On when, and why?"

"Soon. Like next week. I thought we could take a vacation."

"Together?"

"Nah. I thought I'd go to Padre, and you could spend a week at Lake Texoma." He laughed. "Of course together!"

"I'm not sure that's a good idea."

"Why not? We spend nights together here; we'll just be spending them together somewhere else."

"But what if we drive each other bananas? What if you drive *me* bananas? What would we do with Fido? And we both have companies to run."

He shrugged her back onto his shoulder, resettled her snugly into his arms. "It'll work out." He began to rub tiny circles just above her ear. "My secretary thinks she runs my company most of the time, anyway." He rubbed and rubbed. "And you've got Swan."

Ellie jerked away from his caressing hand. "Have you been talking to her? She told you to do that, didn't she?"

"Do what?" Mike looked puzzled.

"It might work on Clement, but it won't on me!"

"Ellie," he said, "I don't know what you're talking about."

"Yes, you—" She stopped, bit her lip and breathed deeply. Of course he didn't know; how could he? His stroking her head must be coincidence.

But she could see how Clement always fell for it. And Swan was right: a bald spot wasn't necessary at all.

"Well," she said, "okay. But I still don't think a vacation's a good idea. Fido's just gotten used to me, to staying here. And Swan would have enough of a burden simply handling the Genies without keeping Fido, too."

"Surely this wouldn't be the first time either of you've taken a vacation. And Fido travels well; she's experienced. We can drive down and find a motel that takes animals."

A motel wouldn't be necessary; her grandfather's beach house should be empty. But Ellie balked at going because until now, they'd only been together for short periods of time. What if he tired of her?

"Come on, Ellie," he prodded her. "You'll enjoy it."

She squeezed her eyes shut and gnawed on her lip. Running from life was no way to live. With Mike, she had finally begun to realize that. So maybe she should try it.

"It would take some juggling..." she said, wavering.

Ten

___

The deserted beach stretched before Ellie, sandy and endless, as she strolled parallel to the water's edge. Fido trotted behind her.

The warmth of the sun seeped through her, touching every part but the emptiness inside her. A sea gull swooped overhead, its lonely cry melting over her silence.

She'd spent three days alone at her grandfather's beach house on Padre Island. And still the silence grew louder.

When a trailer had caught fire at the Dunes well, Mike had insisted that Ellie start their vacation without him, promising that he'd join her in a day or so.

Or three or four.

She scuffed her sandaled feet in the sand, watching it spew up in front of her. Fido darted to one side, leaping after a gnat.

As a child Ellie had stood on the cool, flat sand and dreamed that hers were the only footprints to ever mark this place. She'd studied the unbroken horizon and felt that she was the first to watch the sun stretch over the water and draw shadows on the beach. Back then, in solitude and solemnity, she had claimed this piece of sand and ocean for herself.

Now she reclaimed it, for her and for Fido, as if they were the only creatures in the world.

She kicked at the sand. Before too long she and Fido would have to start back to Dallas, without Mike.

Again a gull screeched. Ellie checked the sky overhead, shielding her eyes from the bright white sun, and frowned. How strange, she thought, that the vacation she'd reluctantly agreed to, she now hated to see end.

Crossing her legs Indian style, she sank onto the sand, leaned against a rock and tweaked the front brim of her straw hat lower as she watched the rhythmic flow of the waves.

Mike had called every night that she'd been there. Not to talk about his problems in Arizona; he evaded her questions about that. Instead, his calls had been poignantly seductive. Though she'd missed him, for a while afterward, she'd carried the glow of him inside her.

Now she extended her legs and scooted further down in the sand. She'd forgotten her towel, but she didn't care. Only the bulk of her French braid cushioned her head on the rock, but that didn't bother her, either.

Fido curled up next to her. Lazily she stroked the cat.

"I think you and I could adjust to being beach bums, Fido," she said.

Fido's ear twitched.

Ellie smiled. The cat was beginning to recognize her name. "Fido?" she said as a test, this time a little louder.

Fido's ear swirled, arcing toward Ellie's voice like a beacon. Maybe soon she'd react to the sound of her name as readily as she did to the whir of the electric can opener.

Ellie was almost dozing when she heard her name over the surf. Blinking, she sat up and listened intently. The call came again, the faint voice unrecognizable.

Maybe she was imagining it. Perhaps it was only the cry of the gulls. Loneliness did strange things to a person.

Then the voice grew clearer. Her name.

When she rose, so did Fido. The cat stretched, her body rippling.

In the distance, Mike waved at them. Ellie ran to him and threw herself at him with abandon.

"You made it," she cried. "I thought you'd never get here. Fido thought you'd never come, too. But here you are. Finally." She kissed his eyes, his cheeks, his forehead, his chin, his jaws. Then finally her mouth captured his.

He groaned, and she felt his body harden against her. Then he raised his head and blew out a whistling sigh. "Give me a second to catch my breath."

"Since when do you need to breathe?" she laughed, stepping away.

He didn't seem to share her amusement. Instead he raked his fingers through his hair and said, "I need to talk to you for a minute. Why don't we go back to the house." He sounded on edge; his manner was distracted.

"Sure." She fell into step beside him, trying to ignore the disquiet within her. He obviously was under some type of stress. She hoped the stress wouldn't affect the few days they had left of their vacation. She wanted their time together to be unpressured, for his sake as much as hers.

"You are staying a few days, aren't you? Fido and I've been having the time of our lives; we'd be glad to share with you. I'm surprised that a cat would adjust to the beach so easily. She stays away from the water, of course, but she's not the least bit intimidated—"

"I really missed you, you know."

Ellie faltered but didn't misstep. "I'm glad," she said brightly. "But at least you had people to talk to. Fido refuses to speak anything but 'cat.'"

Loping along beside Mike, Fido demonstrated. *"Miiaowrr."*

"See?" Ellie said. "And she won't translate. Makes me guess what it means."

He picked up the cat. "I understand her," he said. "That was hello."

Fido purred. Louder, Ellie decided, than she had in the past three days.

"Now she's telling me how much she missed me. Aren't you, girl? What's that?" He bent his ear toward the cat's mouth, then looked up at Ellie. "She says you missed me, too."

"Tattletale," she muttered, glaring at Fido. "Wait till I tell him about the fish head you snitched out of the trash."

Mike raised an inquiring eyebrow. "What was a fish head doing in the trash?"

"What would it be doing anyplace else? You wouldn't expect me to eat it, would you? Fido shouldn't have had it, either. It had bones in it." From the beach, they climbed a long length of stairs that led to a terrace outside the house. "You should have told me last night that you were coming. I could've picked you up at the airport. The door isn't locked; did you go inside?"

"I saw your car in the driveway, so when you didn't answer the doorbell, I assumed you'd gone to the beach."

"Did you *rent* a car? You won't need one." She paused. "Will you?"

Inside the front door, he stopped her. "What's wrong, Ellie? You haven't stopped chattering since I got here. What's the matter?"

She leaned against the doorjamb. "Nothing's wrong with me. What about with you?"

"Nothing wrong but business," he promised. Then he set Fido on the floor and filled his arms with Ellie. "And for as long as possible," he growled on the way to her mouth, "I plan on doing my best to forget all about business."

Later, on the beach, Ellie ran backward, tracking the curve of a Frisbee as it arced. After an earlier swim, she and Mike had been chasing the Frisbee for a while. And now the blasted thing was...falling short.

She swore, flinging herself toward it. She reached out, straining forward. Then her fingertips grazed the plastic edge, and she clung to a handful of air as the Frisbee hit the sand, bounced once and skidded across the beach.

"We still keeping score?" Mike called.

"You only ask that when you're ahead. Yes, we're keeping score, and no, I'm not losing."

"You're not winning, either."

She picked up the disc and bounced it against her thigh. Although neither gardening nor fishing was muscle building, something she'd been doing—Heaven knew what—helped her keep the score even. But Mike had had her practically running her legs to nubs.

She'd show him. Given a little time, she'd have him breathing just as hard as she was.

Anchoring one hand on the Frisbee like a rudder, she tested the arc of the disc twice without releasing it. On the third thrust, she let go, and it lifted, the wind carrying it high and wide, past Mike.

Ellie whooped and leaped into the air like a gazelle. "Game point!" she hollered.

Mike jogged after the Frisbee, picked it up and trotted back. "Says who?" he asked, slowing as he reached her. He looped an arm around her shoulder and tugged her toward him. "You're really a competitor, aren't you?"

"Who, me?"

"I wasn't talking about Fido."

When they reached their umbrella, they found the cat curled up, asleep.

Mike sank onto a towel, pulling Ellie down after him. "I'm kind of competitive myself," he admitted.

"Kind of?"

"Um-hmm." He nuzzled her neck. "Do you think two kind-of-aggressive people like us could make it together?" He nibbled her earlobe.

She twisted her head away. "Make what? World War III?"

"Nope. I mean make a life together, a home."

All the teasing drained out of her. She stared down at her hands as she twisted them together and, inside, her love warred with her reservations.

Of course she wanted to build a life with him. She could make a home in a tent if he'd share it with her.

But what about him?

She knew up-front what she would get with him—knew of his superstitions, of his dreams, everything she needed to know to make a decision—but she had never told him the truth about how her father had died, never admitted her guilt in it.

"Ellie?" He lifted her chin, forcing her to look at him. "It's too soon, isn't it? You don't have to make a decision right now. Just think about it. Stow it right there—" he tapped her braid "—and let the sun cure it until it's ready."

"I'm sitting in the shade," she pointed out, using logic to hide her uncertainty.

"A minor technicality. Besides, those rays are creeping—" he marched his fingertips slowly up her leg "—past that shade, over the sand, up your bathing suit." He lowered his voice until he sounded like a radio announcer on an old horror show. "They're everywhere, and they penetrate . . . everything. Nothing is safe, nothing secure, nothing sacred."

As he talked, he made forays with his fingers, demonstrating the powers of the sun. "Ahh . . . see?" he said, dipping beneath the top edge of her turquoise maillot to tease a hardened nipple. "A ray must've already been here. And here." He slid a strap from her shoulder, baring a breast, then he covered the nipple with his mouth. This time his tongue teased.

Ellie was starving for him, as if it had been years since he'd touched her, instead of merely days. And the softness, the wetness, of his mouth on her short-circuited her logic. She didn't care that they were on the beach, completely unsheltered from all but the direct rays of the sun.

As he adored one breast with his hand, the other with his mouth, she dropped her head back, her lips parting in ecstasy.

A melting heat began to flow through her—the kind of heat that only Mike could create.

Only Mike—a man with fingers like sensing rods that were drawn to the very part of her that needed his attention most.

"You did say this beach is private, didn't you?" he murmured, his mouth moving against the fullness of her breast.

She groaned. "I'm not sure I even care, but it is."

"Good." He skimmed his fingers down her midsection, tugging the bathing suit down with them.

He stroked her, gentle yet rough, sensitive but demanding, then followed the caress of his hands with the brush of his mouth, building in her a driving, compulsive urgency. And she surrounded him with her hands, her thighs, her lips, engulfing him, almost absorbing him. She wanted him to melt into her, wanted to drink him up through her pores.

When he finally slid into her warmth, a fullness spread through her that had nothing to do with the bulk of him. It was coming home and being whole all at the same time.

He made the earth tremble for her. His thrust as he surged into her surely shook the very continent itself.

Higher and higher she spiraled. Out of control, she dug her fingernails into his hips, greedily hanging on, pulling him toward her, merging until together they exploded into a Utopian world, a fantasy that existed now but would soon fade into memory. Until next time.

"It's a good thing we're not on the West Coast," she told him as they dressed. "We'd have probably just quaked California into the Pacific."

They took one last stroll before going in for lunch. As they walked, Ellie stole a glance at Mike's face. "I still can't whistle," she admitted.

"You need to practice, that's all. You were taught by the best."

"Best what? Lover? Gambler? What?"

He hooked her shoulder with his arm. "When I'm with you, I feel like I'm the best at everything, but I was talking about whistling."

"Well, you're not worth beans teaching it. Nobody can curl their tongue; I've taken a survey. No, don't show me how *you* do it. I remember how you do it, but I believe some people can whistle, some can do the splits, some can stand on their heads."

"What can you do?"

"Lots. Like throwing a mean Frisbee."

"Well, try whistling one more time. Do it the way I showed you."

She tried. Her lips pursed beautifully, and her tongue curled part of the way. But the only sound she achieved was a warped raspberry.

Mike chuckled—snidely, if she was any judge.

"That's enough," she said. "Any more practicing will be done in private. Without critics."

With Mike beside her—his dark hair burnished by the sun, his yellow plaid swimsuit showing off his lean, tan body, his stride easy and ambling—the beach had never looked lovelier, nor the sea bluer, nor the sun brighter.

He had asked her to make a life with him, and she wanted to, desperately. And why shouldn't she? Telling him about herself shouldn't be that hard.

"Mike?"

"Hmm?"

"I, uh, well . . . you never did say what happened in Arizona."

Why had she asked that? Sure, she wanted to know, but not right this moment. Right now, more than anything, she needed to tell him about her past. But what she wanted was to spend a few more moments in the security of his love.

"We lost everything in the trailer," he told her, "and were lucky at that. No one was hurt. But that's not what took me so long." He shoved his hands into his pockets. "The authorities have proved it was arson."

"But Mike, why would anyone . . . who would . . . ?"

"Who knows? Maybe someone wanted to watch it burn . . . or maybe they wanted to hurt my company."

"Will it?"

"There'll be an investigation, of course. But aside from the annoyance factor, all we've really lost that's irreplaceable is time." He sighed. "I have a strange feeling . . . I don't know. I guess it's a fear that someone really does want to damage Bannister Drilling. Maybe it's because I've put so much into it."

She slipped her hand into his, and he squeezed it.

"What do you think? You think I should worry?"

A prickly sense of unease gnawed at her. She pulled her hand away. "I think you're probably going to no matter what I say."

"Probably. There are other factors, though."

"Like what?"

"Bannister's stock. For some reason both the volume and the price have picked up in the past month."

"Should that concern you?"

"It didn't until the fire. Maybe it shouldn't even now. What do you think?"

"I'm not a good person to ask. I don't play the market, so I don't know that much about what anything means."

"But you're an intuitive lady. Consider this: a sudden burst of stock activity could mean that a company's coming out with a new product or a merger's anticipated or a change is being made in administration. Basically it either forecasts or follows some major change. And there's been no change in the company."

"So when you put that together with arson...?"

"I don't know...I just don't know." He dragged his fingers through his hair. "Tell me, Ellie, tell me it's my imagination."

"Mike, I can't tell you that! Please don't ask me. If you see disaster, that's your summation, not mine. And if that's what you think, then what the hell are you doing down here? Why aren't you in Dallas, taking care of it?"

"Hey!" He stopped and put his hand on her shoulder. "What's wrong?"

"Just don't ask me to decide anything for you. I don't do that. And don't...don't *not* do things you should be doing because you think I have some kind of intuition. I won't be responsible for it. I won't be responsible for you! Do you hear me?"

"Ellie." His voice was soothing, his hand on her chin placating. "Ellie, I didn't mean to upset you. Tell me what's wrong. What's the matter?"

She jerked her chin away. "I'm not good at responsibility, dammit. I can't, don't you see?"

"I can only see that you're upset." He gripped her shoulders. "What is it? Tell me what's wrong."

"My father, he died because..." Sudden tears flooded her eyes, overflowing and streaming down her cheeks. "Because of me."

"Ellie. God, I'm sorry." Mike enfolded her in his arms, and she began to sob, her words becoming even more disjointed.

"What happened? Tell me."

"I should have known...but I was mad. I was mad, so I didn't come home until, until it was too late. He was—Mike, he was so...white, so cold. But he wasn't dead. Not till later. He tried... There was orange juice all—all down his shirt... He knew what he needed, and he tried...." The old pain, all the old guilt, rocked over her, washing her away again in its icy embrace. "I should've been there," she ended with a final sob.

"But, darling, you were just a child."

She sucked in a shuddering breath. "He counted on me. And I did take care of him. For two years I did. I knew how volatile his diabetes was. And still I disobeyed him." She swallowed, then swallowed again. "Because of my irresponsibility he died. If I'd just gone home like I was supposed to, I could have caught the reaction... before it killed him."

She stepped away from Mike and wiped the tears from her face. "I'd like to go back to the house now," she said.

The next morning, Fido nudged Ellie's ear with a cold nose.

Groaning sleepily on her side, Ellie wrapped an arm around her head, hiding her exposed ear from the cat.

Again Fido nudged, then rubbed the side of her head against Ellie's in one long, smooth movement.

"Go 'way," Ellie muttered.

The cat butted Ellie's chin, purring loudly.

Ellie squeezed her eyes shut and pressed an arm against one ear, her hand over the other, straining to shut out the morning.

Mike lay next to her, his presence soothing both in reality and in her dreams. And her dreams... She tried to recapture that last warm, beautiful one. For just a few more minutes.

Almost her whole head was now hidden by her arm and her pillow. Almost... but not quite.

Fido bit Ellie's nose, firmly but gently.

Ellie's eyes flew open. "Wha...? Fido! What in blazes...?" She sat up. "You little devil!"

Ellie knew that if cats could smile, Fido would have smirked. There was implicit satisfaction in the way that she jumped off the bed and padded toward the bedroom door, looking smugly over her shoulder at Ellie.

"So, okay." Ellie got out of bed. "So you want breakfast. Was that any reason to bite me?"

"Huh?" Mike rolled over, flinging his hand onto the vacant space beside him. "What's the matter?"

"I'm just going to feed Fido," she told him as she put on her robe. "Go back to sleep."

Afterward Ellie sat down at the breakfast bar, crossed her arms on the counter and watched the coffee perk.

She hadn't wanted to admit to Mike that she blamed herself for her father's death. And now that she had, he'd shown her only kindness. But what about later? What about after the first flush of sympathy was gone? When did the horror come, when the realization that she was guilty of something worse than negligence? In anger, she had allowed her father to die.

Try as she might, she couldn't forget the last day of his life. They'd argued at breakfast. He'd told her he had to sell the house because he'd made another bad investment. She'd been angry and frustrated and had felt guilty for that.

Because of her anger, she'd gone to a friend's house after school.

She should have known better. She knew how haphazard he was about his condition. Once a noise awakened her in the night and she discovered her father fumbling beneath the kitchen sink. Even though he was dazed, it was as if he knew he needed food but not where to find it. That time she'd been able to get enough orange juice in him to counteract the hypoglycemia. But more than once she'd found him after the insulin reaction had advanced too far for her to handle it alone and she'd had to call the paramedics for help.

Now she braced her face on her fists, gritting her teeth against the old pain, the old memories.

No amount of recrimination could change what had happened to her father. She'd tried. God knew she had. She'd lashed herself for years with regret over how she'd failed him. But regret couldn't bring him back.

* * *

Later that morning, the air from the ocean blew cool across the deck as the sun cowered behind a cloud of gray. But Ellie's dark mood affected Mike much more than the weather.

"Great breakfast," he said, polishing off the last of his *huevos rancheros*.

She smiled tightly. "Lousy day. But this is the first time it's been cloudy since I've been here."

"I wish I'd made it for the sunshine."

"It'll be back."

"Good," he said. "I'll be ready for it."

"Me, too."

More than the table stretched between them, Mike thought. Somehow, instead of bringing them together, her outburst on the beach yesterday had separated them. But he intended to get past those barriers. He wouldn't let her old pain keep them apart. He'd get her to talk with him; soon she'd tell him where it hurt the worst.

"Would you like some more coffee?" she asked.

"Why don't we get these things cleaned up and go back to the beach? I'd like to see those whitecaps up closer."

He understood old pain, probably better than most people. But he had never before realized how strong, how unresolved, Ellie's was. Together they could mend it, though; together they could stitch up and smooth over yesterday's wounds.

As water filled the sink, he touched Ellie's shoulder. "I love you, you know."

Pain creased her brow, and tears welled in her eyes. He wrapped her in his arms. "We'll work it out," he promised. "Just don't turn away from me. Please."

She nodded tearfully. And his day brightened. He didn't need sunshine as long as he had her smile, soggy as it was.

Then the ring of the telephone shattered the moment.

Ellie answered. "Hello. Yes, um-hmm. Sure, just a minute." She handed the phone to Mike. "It's for you."

"I gave Dixie the number. I hope there aren't any complications at the well." Then, into the receiver, he said, "Hello."

"Hello, Mike," David replied.

"David? What's wrong? Are Mother and Dad—"

"I'm calling about business."

Relief rushed through Mike, then confusion. He was glad there'd been no family disaster but, except for that first year he'd spent at Davis Oil, he and David had never had any business together.

"Business," David went on, "as in Bannister Drilling's annual report. You've made the company look very enticing."

A foreboding grew in Mike. He didn't like the sound of David's statement, but he quelled his aversion, giving David a chance to prove him wrong.

"I want it," David said coldly, confidently.

Mike's anger was directed almost as much at himself as it was at David. He'd actually believed the man was softening, had been suckered into accepting David's amiability.

"Out of the question," he said in a clipped tone. "Bannister Drilling isn't interested in merging with anyone." He didn't add "especially you," but the emotion hung between them, anyway.

"You don't have much choice," said David. "I'm filing with the Securities and Exchange Commission this week. I'll force the merger on you."

So David had caused Bannister Drilling's activity on the stock exchange. "How much of the outstanding stock have you already picked up?"

"Just under the five-percent limit."

Mike's mind raced. David was obviously being careful, playing by the rules. Anyone going after more than five percent of a publicly held stock had to register that intention with the SEC, as David claimed to be doing. That filing would allow him to start hunting down vast quantities of the shares on the open market—until he had enough to gain control of the firm.

"It'll cost me more this way," David allowed, "because I'll have to offer a premium price for your stock."

He paused, and Mike could almost picture his half brother's haughty expression. Not even his childhood icicle fantasy helped him now.

"It'll be worth it in the end," David said. "No matter what price I have to pay, it's going to be worth it to me."

"Is this a payback, David?" Mike didn't expect an honest answer, but he wanted to have as many cards put on the table as he could manage.

"Call it what you will," David said. "Call it debt collecting, if you like. I'm due."

"I'll fight you."

David chuckled. "I would've been disappointed if you didn't. That's what's going to make this encounter so interesting . . . and so satisfying when I win. Because I will, Mike. There's nothing you can do to stop it. One way or another, Bannister Drilling's going to be mine."

Eleven

Ellie sat in Mike's living room, studying the half-finished jigsaw puzzle on the coffee table before her. She picked up a piece of blue sky and turned it this way and that. Finally, with lips pursed, she tried to wedge it into a space. It didn't quite fit. She could force it, of course. She'd done that once or twice.

But jigsaw puzzles were as bad as crosswords. Wrong pieces, like wrong answers, ruined the finished product. Sometimes they made it impossible to finish.

In that respect, life was like a jigsaw puzzle. One wrong answer led to another. *Ad infinitum.*

Somehow the thought wasn't as whimsical to her right now as it should have been, perhaps because she was living a wrong fit, a wrong answer.

Beside Ellie, Fido lifted her head, instantly alert. Then she jumped off the sofa, crossed over to the front door and waited.

So the scrape of a key in the front-door lock came as no surprise to Ellie. Straightening, she smoothed back her hair into its braid and stuck a smile on her face.

"Hi," she said brightly as Mike entered. "How's it going?"

The tension that was etched into his face lessened somewhat when he saw her. Maybe she wasn't living such a wrong fit, after all. Perhaps spending as much time here as she had these past three days hadn't really been the wrong answer.

"I've got dinner on the stove," she said, rising to accept his kiss. "Think you could eat something?"

His lips brushed against her cheek. "I might be able to."

"You look tired," she told him on the way to the kitchen. "Actually you look exhausted. I really do understand how much saving your company means to you, but you can't kill yourself over it."

"Needs must when the devil drives," he said with a shrug. "And if Satan's not driving now, it's a damned close relative."

Ellie hadn't intended to complain, had known it would do no good. But she was concerned. The only way she'd been able to see Mike since they'd returned had been to stay here with him. She'd practically given up her own personal life to keep from worrying herself sick over him.

At least here she could make sure he ate one meal a day. Or try, anyway.

She'd hidden too long from the fact that life was filled with responsibilities. She couldn't hide any longer. One couldn't love and escape them, and—like it or not—she loved Mike. Like it or not, she felt responsible for him.

She didn't like it, especially since the responsibility she felt didn't make a whit of difference to Mike's well-being.

He picked at the beef Stroganoff that she'd warmed in the microwave for him.

"Have you decided what your defense will be?" she asked.

He abandoned his food. "Decided, but who knows if it'll work."

"You said these lawyers specialized in hostile takeovers, and so does the financial firm you hired. Don't you trust their advice?"

"It's not that easy. Sure, there are strategies we could use that would almost guarantee a win, of sorts. David doesn't want Bannister Drilling. He wants to ruin me. And if I strip my company to win it, who wins then?"

"What about your father?"

"This isn't Dad's fight. It's between David and me, period." He smiled totally without humor. "And Dad couldn't make much difference, anyway. He signed over most of his shares of Davis Oil to David and Sarah before he left for Monaco. He didn't retain enough to give himself a voice in the company's operation. Between them, David and Sarah hold the controlling shares of Davis Oil."

She could understand the frustration he must be feeling. Every way he turned seemed to be blocked. "So what defense are you going to use?" she asked.

He leaned back and pushed his plate away. "It's called self-tender. We're going to make the same offer per share that David has." He shook his head. "It's a gamble. We're hoping that I'll be considered a known quantity and will that way pull in more shares."

"But you're worried."

"Hell, yes. I don't want to lose the company, either way. But if I let it die, I affect a lot more people than if I let it go. I just don't want to do either, so I'm trying to stack the cards in my favor as much as possible." He squeezed her hand. "Having you here helps. A lot. Anyway, tomorrow we make our offer, and after that, who knows?"

He worked the rest of that evening on the papers he'd brought home from the office. After finishing her puzzle, Ellie read for a while. Every now and then she caught herself falling asleep over her book, and she'd jerk awake, growing more irritable each time Mike suggested she go to bed without him.

At three o'clock, he shook her awake. "Come on," he said. "Let's go to bed."

In bed, sleep vanished. She lay there, wide-eyed, listening to him breathe.

Finally he said, "Can't you sleep?"

"Not now. How about you?"

"Me, either. Come here, why don't you?"

She scooted across the bed and laid her head on his shoulder. "Are you worrying?"

"It doesn't do much good, I know. But I can't seem to stop."

"Did your advisers give odds on your chances for success? I mean like which strategy would be your best bet?"

"That's the reason I went with the one I did. All things considered, it was the best. What do you think, Ellie? What would you suggest?"

Her breath knotted in her throat. What did she think? She thought his best bet was never to listen to her suggestions.

"I don't even know what the choices were."

"Well, first—"

"Mike—" she covered his mouth with her hand "—you're paying for good advice. Those men are experts. I'm lucky I find my way to work in the morning."

He pulled her hand down to his chest. "Just pretend someone was trying to take over the Genies and these were your choices of defense."

Briefly he outlined the basics of each type, and her head spun with the sound of them. Some seemed even more bizarre than others, and those were the ones she remembered: the poison pill, the white knight and the golden parachute.

"So," he said, "what do you think? If you were me, which one would you use?"

"The poison pill," she muttered. "Suicide has to be the only way out. No, seriously, I could make better suggestions at the racetrack, and we both know how I am there."

"I'm not asking you to choose for me," he told her patiently. "Maybe I'm just looking for reassurance."

"Well, then, in that case, tomorrow I'd do exactly what you're doing: listen to the experts. Tonight, well..." She cuddled closer. "Tonight's a different matter altogether."

Three and a half weeks later, early on a Tuesday morning, Ellie watched the hands on the kitchen clock march steadily onward. Mike hadn't come home until three o'clock and was sleeping now. He'd asked to be awakened at six. Too short a time, too long a time.

She felt as if she'd been waiting all night long, first for Mike to come home, now for him to get up. Weariness dragged her eyelids, but she knew she couldn't sleep. She needed to get Mike up on time.

She was thankful that he'd been willing to try to rest at all. He'd lost weight throughout this ordeal, and his face was drawn with exhaustion.

Before he'd slept, though, he'd told her where the situation stood. It wasn't good. There were seventy-two hours still left in the self-tender offer, and the company was substantially short of the shares it needed to withstand the takeover attempt. Mike's advisers held out little hope for a win.

Now slowly, inexorably, time crept on.

Ellie dug the heels of her hands into her brow. Why? Why should it come to this? Who was to blame for it? Life? Fate? God? Ellie herself?

Mike had told her once that Bannister Drilling had been his strength against a world where he felt he had no strength. It was his underpinnings, his affirmation that he was worth every bit as much as his siblings.

And now it was gone, irretrievably gone.

Could she have stopped it? Surely not. It was vengeance on David's part. That had nothing to do with her; that had to do with Ed and Audrey and Lucinda and a time before Ellie had even been born.

So why did she feel so damned responsible? Tears leaked from her eyes, puddled in her heart. Could she have changed it? What if he'd tried a white knight? Or a poison pill? Why hadn't she checked somewhere to at least find out more about each one?

But no. "Listen to the experts," she'd told him. Well, who in blazes said the experts knew it all? He probably should have gotten a second opinion. Somebody else's second opinion, not hers.

But why had she thought things would be different with Mike? What insanity had made her believe that she could love him and not hurt him? Her experience should have warned her that in this imperfect world, love sometimes caused hurt.

Fido flicked a paw against her cheek, and she hugged the cat. She'd resisted taking Fido, when she should have been resisting her love for Mike. She was a curse. There were no two ways about it. She was a curse to anyone she loved, anyone who loved her back.

She swallowed a sob and stood, wiping her face with the back of her hands. The digital clock on the microwave read 5:45. With her emotions still churning, Ellie tried to still her jangled nerves by faking normality. She put the water-decaffeinated coffee Mike preferred on to perk and dropped a slice of rye bread, his favorite, into the toaster. Since he refused to sit down to breakfast, perhaps he'd eat while he dressed....

Before the toaster even popped, Mike strode into the kitchen, wide-awake, fully dressed and freshly shaven.

Ellie grimaced a tear-streaked smile. "Good morning. Feeling better?"

He nodded as he poured his coffee into his travel mug. Then he squinted a glance at his watch.

Like Alice's rabbit, she thought. She wouldn't have been surprised to see Mike's ears wiggle or to hear him bemoan how late he was.

"Sit down and drink your coffee." She slathered peanut butter on the toast. "You're up earlier than you meant to be, so you should have time for breakfast."

"I really don't." He stirred three teaspoonfuls of sugar into his coffee. "I need to get into the office. I've got plenty to do."

"At least take this with you," she said, spreading on jelly. "You can eat it as you drive."

She wasn't sure if he really wrinkled his nose as she held out the toast, or if that was simply her imagination. What he said was "I'll send Dixie out for doughnuts after I get to the office."

All her fears and anger seemed to converge, boiling up inside her. She looked from the toast to Mike, then back at the toast again. She wasn't doing a damn bit of good for him here, never had, never would.

"So don't eat it." She slammed the toast onto the countertop, jelly side down. "Don't eat anything, and see if I care."

He winced. "I'm sorry, Ellie. I know I haven't been the easiest person in the world to live with—"

"Try impossible. And I've had it up to here." She hit her chin with the side of her hand. "I've done everything I could for you, Mike, and it's not enough. What do you want from me, for God's sake?"

"Ellie?"

His look of confusion fueled her anger. "You want a good-luck charm, don't you? Well, I told you I wasn't one, but did you listen? No-o-o. You asked my advice, anyway. 'What should I do, Ellie?'" she mimicked prissily. "'What would you do if you were me?' Well, I sure as hell wouldn't have asked my advice!"

"Now's not a good time, Ellie—"

"My father depended on me, and I told you what happened to him. You knew I couldn't be counted on, so why did you?" She parked her hands on her hips and leaned forward. "If you hadn't put so damned much faith in me, I couldn't have failed you. I warned you I'm no good when the chips are down. If you'd listened to me and *not* listened to me, you might just still have your company."

Mike had begun to look irritated. "Don't you think you're being unreasonable?" he asked in a maddeningly reasonable tone.

"And you're not? Oh, no, you're Mr. Perfect, Mr. Logical Bannister. And I'm *il*logical, *ir*responsible and *un*reasonable. Well, that should come as no surprise; I tried to tell you. Did you think I was pretending to feel guilty about my father? I *was* guilty, dammit! I was the one who gave him his shots and made sure he ate on time. He was *my* responsibility. And now you—" She choked on her rising hysteria, trying desperately to compose herself. How could she make him understand when she couldn't even talk?

But the tears kept on coming. Blindly she gestured a staying motion with the flat of her hand, then she flung herself out of the kitchen and into the bedroom, where she buried her face in her hands and fought her sobs.

She expected him to follow her, hoped he would, needed him to. The security of his embrace could have worked miracles.

Instead he left, without a word.

Two hours later she sat at her desk in the office. She hadn't accomplished a thing this morning, couldn't even think about work.

She fiddled with her folded glasses. She realized now that by blowing up this morning she'd been trying to abdicate. The tension of the past three weeks, coupled with the burden of Mike's pain and the guilt of her own misguided advice, had her going in circles.

She couldn't have love without responsibility; she knew that. And she'd just seen the results of her inability to handle responsibility. So what was she to do now? How could she continue to care for Mike, knowing the price he might have to pay for that caring?

She needed to think, needed to decide. Dammit, she needed to go somewhere where she could think without all the pressure.

But first she had to apologize. Obviously Mike couldn't fathom her fear of responsibility, so how could he understand her state of mind? She had to at least try to explain.

Swiftly she punched out his office number. Dixie answered on the first ring.

"Mike's not available right now." Then her voice lowered, though it remained clear, as if she were whispering with her mouth close to the receiver. "He's with his sister. That condescending witch has come to gloat; I just know it. She never gave him a moment's notice before.'' Dixie paused, breathed in, then blew it out angrily. ''I'd punch her lights out for her, only it'd probably make things worse for Mike.''

Obviously Ellie's scene this morning had led into another, this one probably more difficult. Her sense of guilt increased tenfold. Her feelings of responsibility, too.

''Do you think it would help if I came over?'' she asked.

To Ellie's ears, Dixie's hesitation took on the amplitude of a drumroll.

''Mike's . . . going to be kind of busy today. He's asked me to reschedule all his appointments. But,'' Dixie added hurriedly, ''why don't I ask him? I'm sure he'd like to see you.''

''That's all right. I'll be pretty busy, too. But Dixie . . . watch out for him, okay?''

That afternoon at Swan's cabin, the sun floated low in the sky, its rays radiating off the surface of the lake. The summer heat hung heavy and stifling, and not even the slightest breeze blew off the water.

Ellie had come alone, except for Fido. Now, in baggy shorts, a T-shirt and an old baseball hat of Clement's, she sat on the bank, shaded by the foliage of an oak tree. She'd been here for a couple of hours now, and all she and Fido had done was walk for a while, then sit for a while. Now Fido leaped after butterflies, but still Ellie sat.

Try as she might, she hadn't reached a decision.

The facts were easy to enumerate. She loved Mike. And she couldn't imagine a life without him, didn't want to even try. But he put too much stock in her opinion.

He loved her; she felt sure of that. Together they'd been better than she'd ever thought they could be.

But she'd cost him his business.

He probably wouldn't allow her to leave him—if he knew she was doing it for his sake.

Still this time it had been his livelihood. What might she cost him next?

Fireflies dotted the darkness as night crept around her. Mosquitoes fed, yet Ellie ignored them. She'd sat under the same tree, in the same position, for hours now, leaning against the trunk, her legs stretched before her.

She'd crumpled her baseball cap in her hands, her fingers mindlessly snapping and unsnapping the plastic back, pulling the cap into an ever smaller circumference, much like the band around her heart that squeezed tighter and tighter.

Two thoughts raged within her, two ideas, dissonant yet inescapable.

She had to leave Mike, but how could she? Her world held nothing without him. Only with him had she managed to grab happiness for the first time in her life; only with him had she felt truly whole.

Digging her fingers into the crumpled cap, she brought it to her trembling lips. She faced the simplest choice she'd ever have to make—and the most difficult. She loved Mike too much to stay with him— that part was simple. But life without him would be the hard part. Without him, each moment she lived for the rest of her life would feel interminable.

The sounds of evening ebbed and flowed around her without her notice. Then tires screeched on tarmac and a shout followed.

Frowning, she peered sharply into the shadows around her. Where was Fido? How long had it been since she'd last seen the cat?

"Fido!" She stood. "Fido!"

From the start Fido had answered to a call only when she wanted to. But when she didn't come, Ellie began to worry. There wasn't a great deal of traffic around this part of the lake, but it didn't take a lot of traffic to cause disaster. One car was plenty.

"Fido," Ellie called again, struggling through the darkness on her way back to the cabin. In the darkness, she stumbled over biting briars, waded through thick underbrush. With each step her concern grew.

"But Fido'll be all right," she assured herself. "She's waiting at the back of the cabin. Hungry as the devil."

The time for food had long passed. Already it was almost midnight. But no cat stood by the back door, nor by the front.

After turning the outside lights on and locating a flashlight, she began to search the area near the cabin, the area from which the screeching tires had come. Then, calling for Fido, she wandered the twisting streets, shining the light into every patch of shrubbery, sweeping each side of the road with it.

With every step, her certainty grew. Fido carried her own sense of time. Ellie could almost set her clocks by the cat's demand for food. Fido wouldn't have run away until at least after dinner.

And why should Fido escape Ellie's curse? She loved the cat, dammit. Fido was hers, not lent, not visiting for a while. Fido was hers, and now she was gone, like everyone else Ellie had ever loved, like even Mike would be...soon.

Still Ellie walked. She trudged the streets, as if by refusing to give up she could weigh the balance in Fido's favor. And she alternated between calling Fido's name and praying. "Please, God, please."

Several times her path brought her back to the cabin. Finally, exhausted, she sank onto the porch steps. Fido was gone. If the kitten had been alive, been where she could hear Ellie, she would have shown herself.

All Ellie's sorrow welled in her. This one last tragedy was too much to bear, and now she mourned not just Fido but everything she'd lost. The tears streaked down her face. She cried for Fido. She cried for her father, for Mike, for herself, for the times that never were and never would be. She cried as if each painful spasm unlocked a desperate knowledge that she had hidden all her life, the knowledge of the curse she was and always would be. She cried freely, with no restraint.

She cried so hard that she didn't hear the sound at first. But finally, it sank in: a faint meow was coming from somewhere nearby.

Still snuffling, Ellie listened harder. It seemed to be coming from under her. She knelt on the ground beside a vent in the pier-and-beam foundation. "Fido?"

"Miiaowrr!" Fido's cry was a little stronger now. She was under there, under the house.

But how had she gotten there? And how could Ellie get her out?

She walked around the house, shining her flashlight along the foundation until, on the side, she found an opening. Sticking her head inside, she called Fido. The cat's answer was distant, faint.

She poked her flashlight inside, and the light sliced through the darkness, illuminating the multiple beams that supported the cabin.

Squelching her aversion to spiders and rats, Ellie crawled through. Again she called; again Fido answered faintly.

Cobwebs brushed her face, and she shuddered. But she crawled on, following the sound of Fido's meow. After she'd traveled approximately a quarter of the length of the cabin, she stopped and again swept her light over the area.

Calmly Fido ambled toward her, looking more than a little bedraggled, her fur matted with cobwebs and dust. Then she meowed and rubbed against Ellie.

"What was your problem?" Ellie demanded tearfully. "Why didn't you come when I called?"

Fido said nothing, so Ellie led the way out. Once they'd crawled out of the darkness, she hugged the cat joyfully. Fido bore the embrace for a moment, then began to wiggle. Enough, she seemed to say, was enough.

Inside, as Fido feasted on a can of tuna, Ellie sat on the corner of the couch.

A new factor had been added to her equation.

She hadn't wanted to love Fido, but she did, hadn't wanted to love Mike, but Heaven knew she loved him, too. She loved him so desperately that she wasn't complete without him. So what in God's sweet name was she doing here?

"Protecting him," she whispered into the darkness, her voice softly asserting.

But had leaving him saved his company? Of course not. Somewhere right now Mike was alone, without Bannister Drilling and without Ellie. He'd had to go through the worst alone, because she was a coward.

She dropped her head back and stared into the darkness overhead, trying to recall the justification that had carried her here.

What if? What if she had suggested Mike get a second opinion on his defense strategy? What if she'd suggested nothing? What if she'd simply stood by him and kept her mouth shut?

She could what-if herself until Satan wore icicles without changing a thing that had happened. She'd given Mike a reasonable answer—an answer that most anyone would have given.

Even so, she should have known better than to become involved with him in the first place, should've known better than to fall in love. If she hadn't, he wouldn't have asked her advice, and she wouldn't have given it. And she wouldn't feel so responsible watching him lose everything he had in the world.

But he still would have lost it. David's takeover had nothing to do with her. If she'd never met Mike, he would be right where he was this minute: without the company and without her. But she wouldn't have left a void then; he wouldn't have even noticed she wasn't there.

She closed her eyes over a sudden realization. Giving advice to Mike wasn't where she'd failed him.

She'd failed him when she ran away. Love *was* responsibility; there was no avoiding that fact. The only way to hide from responsibility was to hide from life, to live in a vacuum.

Life without Mike would be worse than a vacuum; she would have no life without him.

The years before she'd met him might have been safe enough, but they'd been lonely. And as long as she still had a choice, she'd rather face any risk than return to that loneliness. As long as she had a choice...

With a desperation born of fear, she gathered Fido, her purse and her car keys and started back to Dallas in the gray of predawn.

She clenched the steering wheel on the way back, pushing the car, pushing her luck. And the hum of the wheels teased her, their repetition taunting. What if... what if...

What if he didn't want her back? What if *he* blamed her, too? He'd said he would accept his own responsibility, but what if he didn't?

By the time she reached Dallas, the rising sun layered the sky with pink and purple and gold. Anxiety rode her as she pulled in front of Mike's house and, leaving Fido in the car for the moment, she ran to the door.

Fumbling with the keys, she unlocked the door and stepped in. "Mike," she called. "Where are you?"

There was no answer.

As she wandered through the empty house, guilt tugged at her. She should have been here with him last night. He wouldn't give up until he had to, but she knew these next couple of days were going to be hell for him.

Back in the car, she rested her head against the wheel, fighting her tears. She'd experienced a setback, not a defeat.

She took Fido to her house and called Mike's office. The service answered. "Mr. Bannister isn't expected in until nine," they informed her.

She gathered what fortitude she could and waited until a more reasonable hour. By eight o'clock she could wait no longer. Whether or not he was taking calls, Mike surely would be in his office now.

She drove directly to the Davis Building and climbed the stairs. Dixie sat at her desk. She wasn't wearing the long face Ellie would have imagined.

"Hi," Dixie said brightly. "Was Mike expecting you? He's in a meeting now, but he should be through soon if you want to wait."

When he came out, he swept a cold glance over her and shook hands with an older gentleman. Then the man was gone.

"Could I talk with you?" Ellie asked nervously.

Mike seemed distant as he ushered her into his office. And why not? She had run away when the chips were down.

Standing inside the closed door, she cleared her throat. "I, uh, I'm sorry I left the way I did."

He shrugged and crossed to his desk. "When the going gets tough..."

"It wasn't like that," she blurted.

He looked so cold, so untouchable. She wrung her hands in front of her. How could she reach him, how make him understand?

She had to try, whether he finally turned away or not.

"Mike, it was almost like temporary insanity. You put so much stock in me as your good-luck charm, I just got scared when everything soured, and I ran away." She added quickly, "But I'm not running now. I love you and I'll take whatever responsibility comes with that. I don't care *why* you need me, even if it's only as a good-luck charm. I just hope you still *do* need me."

He sat on the edge of his desk and swept a glance over her. His gray eyes chilled her with their intensity. "I don't need you," he said. "I never did."

She sucked in a painful breath, fighting the tears that scalded her eyes. Of course he didn't need her. How could she have believed otherwise? She turned to go.

"I haven't lost the company."

His words stayed her, midturn.

"Sarah saved it," he went on. "She carried enough of the Bannister stock in her name to swing the balance." He gave a rueful laugh. "She didn't do it because she's crazy about me or because all of a sudden she's proud to be my sister. She just didn't like the scandal David was causing with the takeover."

A wave of thankfulness washed over Ellie. She didn't care about Sarah's reasons; she only cared about Mike. And, even though she no longer had him, at least he had his company.

He picked up a pencil from his desk and tapped it against his knuckles. "Sarah and I will never be friends, no matter what Dad would like to think. But it doesn't bother me any longer. I don't need David and Sarah." The pencil stilled. "I don't need you, either. I could probably manage to live quite well without you." Then he said, not tragically but as if finishing a quite ordinary conversation, "But it would be much easier to be dead."

As if the sun had elbowed through a cloud cover, the whole world brightened for Ellie. Murmuring his name, she flung herself into his arms.

And he planted a soul-stirring kiss on her lips. For Ellie, his kiss made the earth tremble. For her, whole universes exploded under the thrill of his embrace.

* * * * *

Silhouette Desire®

1989
IS THE YEAR
OF THE MAN!

What makes a romance? A special man, of course, and Silhouette Desire celebrates that fact with *twelve* of them! From Mr. January to Mr. December, every month has a tribute to the Silhouette Desire hero—our **MAN OF THE MONTH!**

Sexy, macho, charming, irritating . . . irresistible! Nothing can stop these men from sweeping you away. Created by some of your favorite authors, each man is custom-made for pleasure—*reading* pleasure—so don't miss a single one.

Mr. January is Blake Donavan in RELUCTANT FATHER by Diana Palmer
Mr. February is Hank Branson in THE GENTLEMAN INSISTS by Joan Hohl
Mr. March is Carson Tanner in NIGHT OF THE HUNTER by Jennifer Greene
Mr. April is Slater McCall in A DANGEROUS KIND OF MAN by Naomi Horton
Mr. May is Luke Harmon in VENGEANCE IS MINE by Lucy Gordon
Mr. June is Quinn McNamara in IRRESISTIBLE by Annette Broadrick

And that's only the half of it—
so get out there and find your man!

Silhouette Desire's

MAN OF THE MONTH . . .

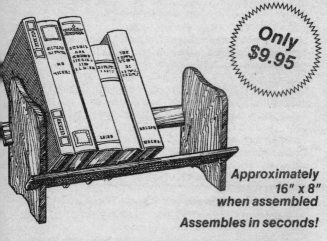

Silhouette Desire ®

COMING NEXT MONTH

AVAILABLE NOW: